Ada,

The Golden Horseshoe

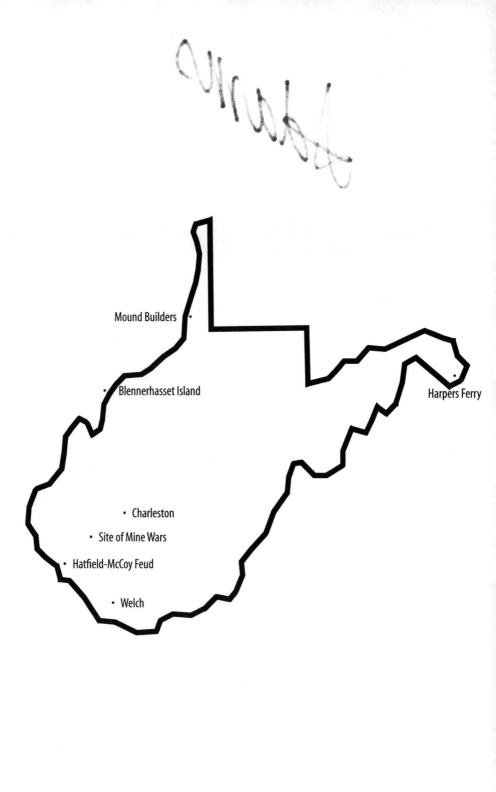

Mound Builders •

• Blennerhasset Island

Harpers Ferry

• Charleston

• Site of Mine Wars

• Hatfield-McCoy Feud

• Welch

The Golden Horseshoe

Frances B. Gunter

ELK RIVER
PRESS

Charleston, West Virginia

Elk River Press
Charleston, WV 25302

ISBN-13: 978-0-9710389-1-2
ISBN-10: 0-9710389-1-0
Library of Congress Number: 2003100059

10 9 8 7 6 5 4 3

Printed in United States of America

Book and Cover Design: Mark S. Phillips
Photography: Ron Gunter

Distributed by:

West Virginia Book Company
1125 Central Avenue
Charleston, WV 25302

www.wvbookco.com

Table of Contents

To Ron, Vivian, and Ronda

Chapter 1

Home to West Virginia

The movie was over. Everyone but Mom was putting away headsets and trying to readjust the multicolored seats. I touched her elbow and she jumped, but she wasn't crying this time. She gazed around her. Without a word she took off the headset and stuffed it in the seat pocket in front of her. She mumbled something about trying to get some sleep and snuggled against the window of the plane.

When I got up last Saturday morning, my only thoughts were about the softball tournament. My game started at 1:30, and the coach had me playing first and batting third. All-stars would be voted on after the game and I had a good chance of being selected. I had done a pretty good job at first base and I seemed to have a hot bat during the tournament. Being the coach's daughter didn't hurt either. I knew Mom would miss the first part of my game, because she was flying home from West Virginia. Grandpa had died, and Mom attended the funeral alone. Since all of us visited last summer and at Christmas, we didn't make the trip last week.

The game went well. My bat wasn't all that great, but I did make the out that won the game. Before the seventh inning all the team members agreed to cast votes only for the three twelve-year-olds on our team. I just knew I would make the all-star team. It was after we got home that Dad broke the news to me. Mom wanted to go back and spend several weeks with Grandma in West Virginia, and he thought I should go with her. My older brother David would be working at a construction site, and I would be home alone during the day if I stayed behind. I argued that I would keep all the doors locked, stay at Aunt Sue's next door, do any laundry, and even try to fix dinner. But nothing worked. Mom and Dad had decided I would return with her to West Virginia. Mom explained

1

that I was Grandma's favorite and Grandma wanted me to come. Dad said I would be doing him a favor by looking after Mom. The truth is, they didn't think I could look after myself. So it was Softball–0 and West Virginia–35.

Forty-eight hours later I was sitting on a 747 bound for Chicago. The turkey croissant, Unity Airway's definition of a light lunch, was jammed back into the serving tray, but the Coke was gladly received. The peanut M & M's would have to do until we landed and I found a Mickey D's to get a burger and fries.

Mom wasn't really sleeping; she just had her eyes closed. I'm not sure if she was thinking about Dad and David at home, Grandpa's death, or helping Grandma after we arrived. At least she wasn't crying, and I had a chance to look around. Our section of the plane, behind first class, had three rows of seats. The muted brown and orange seats were clustered in sets of three, four, and three. We were lucky; we had window seats, and our aisle gave us extra leg room. The stewardesses would usually ask where I was going and offer me magazines to read or puzzles to work.

The pilot announced we would be landing within four minutes, and the seatbelt lights flashed on. Mom stirred and fastened her seatbelt. "We don't need to fool with the luggage here," she said. "If you're hungry, I think we have time to get you a burger in the airport snackbar."

"Doesn't matter," I said, shrugging. "I can wait. It's really no big deal. David wanted a Cubs' T-shirt, and we only have thirty-five minutes. Let's get the shirt." I really didn't care if my brother ever got a Cubs' shirt or not, but I had promised Kim, my best friend, I would get one for her. I knew once we found them I could talk Mom into letting me buy an extra one.

The landing was smooth, and all of the passengers got up at once. Three hundred and forty-two adults stood stoop-shouldered, struggling with carryon packages and totes. If everyone remained seated and left one row at a time, the way school bus drivers scream at kids to do, it would have been much easier. I played adult and stood fifteen minutes before getting into the aisle to leave the plane.

From the hall we entered the Unity terminal and stepped onto the people mover. Overhead the neon tubes of orange, red, blue, and yellow reminded me more of a MTV video than an airport terminal. Since we only had twenty minutes left, we headed to the nearest souvenir shop to

2

look for shirts. I spotted the one I liked immediately, but Mom started reading the wash labels and checking prices. Next came the parent trap.

"Why not wait until the trip home to buy the shirts?" she asked. "They'll just be in the way and take up room at your grandmother's," Mom gave me the typical parent answer number 37.

"Sure we will," I grunted.

"Get the shirts," she snapped. "I don't want to be bothered with this now. Just get them and come on."

This was not what I wanted. I didn't mean to upset Mom; she just seemed so jumpy lately. "No, that's okay. Can I get some M & M's before the next flight? I think they are starting to board," I added quickly.

"Ginny, would you make up your mind, dear. I don't mean to sound angry, but if your grandmother . . ."

I assured her, "It's all right, Mom. We'll get them on the way back. Let's start for the plane."

We hurried through the terminal—this time the neon lights didn't seem as bright—and onto the plane. This plane was much smaller, crowded, and noisy. All the seats were filled and the aisles were small. The stewardesses couldn't help touching the arm rests as they moved up and down the aisles. We had window seats again, so we settled in comfortably. Seatbelt and no-smoking lights came on. The stewardesses had to explain twice to a passenger about putting out a cigarette before we could take off. Finally, we were in the air headed toward Charleston, West Virginia. This short one hour flight brought us to Yeager Airport and Uncle Ron.

Uncle Ron, Mom's brother, was waiting for us inside the terminal. He was my favorite uncle. He could say the right things to Mom to cheer her up, and he was always willing to take Chelsea, Brad, and me anywhere we wanted to go. Aunt Fran gave me a quick hug, while Mom and Uncle Ron embraced. She explained that my cousin Chelsea was already at Grandma's, and Brad was going to summer school at WVU and would visit on weekends. Aunt Fran was okay, for a school teacher, that is. She made good brownies and lasagna, but you *never, never* wanted to start her talking about history. She would bore you to death. Aunt Fran had some snapshots of Chelsea and Brad on a white water rafting trip. I looked at these, while Uncle Ron and Mom went to get our bags.

Chelsea, Brad, and I certainly didn't look like first cousins. I had my Dad's strawberry blonde hair and green eyes, while my cousins had thick, dark brown hair, and brown eyes. Chelsea was two years older, but we were both about five feet two inches, and the same weight. Brad, whose picture I carried (I told everyone he was my boyfriend) was nineteen, tall and well-built. He was on the swim team at WVU and seemed to me to be perfect in every way.

"Hey, you two, let's go!" shouted Uncle Ron, as he waved Aunt Fran and me toward the blue car in the waiting zone at the airport.

Mom was already seated up front, so Aunt Fran and I climbed into the back seat. I knew I would be in for a long two-to-three-hour trip to Grandma's. Aunt Fran would be sure to tell me more than I wanted to know about West Virginia. Sure enough, before we got away from the airport she started.

"Do you know about Chuck Yeager?" she asked.

I was ready for that one. "Oh yes, he flew the first jet to break the sound barrier." I was proud of my answer, but that didn't stop her.

"It's ironic that the airport was named after him. For a while state airport authorities wouldn't allow him to fly in West Virginia because of his crazy stunts. He once flew under the Kanawha Bridge and loved to clip off antennas on top of the houses in Hamlin," she said in her school teacher voice. "He made several trips a year to Hamlin in Lincoln County to visit his mother. The town named a high school after him and erected a monument in his honor. But I'm sure you've heard of him in California."

I was always uneasy when Aunt Fran told me these things, because I was afraid she would give me a test later and I might get an *F*. My dad laughed hysterically one day when I told him this, while Mom just reminded me to be polite to my elders. I guess that meant "listen to Aunt Fran."

"Yes, I heard . . . "

"Oh, look!"

"Where?" I jumped as I turned around, expecting to see something catastrophic.

"There's the Capitol," said Aunt Fran.

Now I know she had seen this Capitol a blue million times, but only a teacher could get excited about a building. I knew my next lesson was coming.

"Did you know . . . " she began.

These three words seemed to be her favorite so I would be hearing them all summer. I began to realize just how much I would miss my dumb brother, my best friend Kim, and even Dad.

4

Without waiting for me to answer Aunt Fran exclaimed, "West Virginia's first real capital was Wheeling, then Charleston, back to Wheeling, and again to Charleston in 1885. The people of the state voted and settled the matter in 1877. This building with the gold dome wasn't built until 1931. The dome is even higher than the one on the U.S. Capitol by five feet, seven and one-half inches. It is also gold-leafed; that means melted liquid gold was applied in a thin layer over the dome."

"Oh," I mumbled.

"It was designed by Cass Gilbert and the style is known as Italian Renaissance."

Uncle Ron came to my rescue. "Hey, give Ginny a break, school is out for the summer. I'm sure she is more interested in the plans Chelsea has for her."

Now I knew why Uncle Ron was my favorite. This slowed Aunt Fran down, and I had an opportunity to look at the mountains as we drove across the turnpike toward Princeton.

At times all I could see were the sides of mountains. The sky would vanish for a short time and then reappear only through the front window. It was cooler in the midst of narrow mountain cuts and much quieter than in Los Angeles. Freeways with eight lanes of traffic were nonexistent in this part of the country. There were a lot of Indian names-like Kanawha, Mingo, Logan, Powhatan, Seneca, Allegheny, Appalachian, and Pocatalico.

Uncle Ron left the turnpike in Princeton, and we turned onto a two-lane highway toward Bluefield and Welch. This stretch of road was like a video game. He was making hairpin turns, and it seemed as if cars and trucks in the opposite lane were coming right toward us. There were a few straight stretches where he would veer into the left lane and pass slower cars in front of us. I held my breath. I forgot about being hungry. In fact, the car seemed to be getting warm, and I didn't feel too well. I tried to read the names of the little towns and coal camps along the way: Bluefield, Bramwell, Maybeury, Elkhorn, Powhatan, Landgraft, Keystone, Kimball, and finally Welch. The old, run-down buildings seemed to push against the road. Bright-colored flowers imprisoned in boxes were the only cheerful signs I could see. Houses appeared along the sides of the mountains, but I couldn't see the roads to reach them. The houses looked like they would slide off the mountainside at any moment. The yards looked green, but the homes and buildings looked

5

drab and tired. Uncle Ron made a sharp right turn, and I recognized the new hospital on the left. We would soon be at Grandma's.

The small brick house with its red tile porch and black wrought iron trim was set between two larger homes, all in a neat row. Another sharp right turn put the car in the driveway, and Uncle Ron stopped in front of the garage. Grandma was sitting on the back porch that ran the length of the house. She didn't look as good as she had last Christmas. She seemed much thinner and her hair looked whiter. She wore her usual white blouse and straight skirt, which always made me wonder what she might look like in a pair of jeans or shorts.

"It's so good to see you," she said warmly as she tried to hug Mom and me at the same time. "How was the trip? I hope Gardner and David didn't mind you coming back so soon."

"No, no, not at all," Mom assured her. "The trip went well, no problems."

"I'm glad I got to come back," I lied. "I don't mean I'm glad about Grandpa . . . I mean I'm glad to come visit you." I'd blown it already. I just knew everyone would start to cry again.

Uncle Ron reached for my arm. "How about you going with me to pick up Chelsea? I think she's at the pool."

"Sounds good," I said.

I got into the front seat next to Uncle Ron, and he gave me a warm smile. "Your grandmother understood what you meant; don't worry about it."

"I didn't know what to say. I'm not happy he died," I whispered, "but I didn't like seeing him sick all the time. He just coughed and coughed. He couldn't sleep, and he made those funny breathing sounds. Does Grandma cry a lot like Mom?"

"No, she doesn't. She saw Dad suffer each day. We all miss him, but it is normal to die. Now let's get on to happier events," Uncle Ron said, as he turned the car into Frank's Dairy Bar. "How about some hot dogs and blizzards before we pick up that daughter of mine?"

"Okay, but let's get something for Chelsea, too," I said.

Uncle Ron answered, "Be my guest. You order."

He handed me a ten dollar bill, and I went up to the window. It was about three o'clock, so there was no line. I had to make up my mind quickly, so I ordered my favorites for all three of us. "Three foot-long hot dogs with everything, that means slaw, too, and three M & M blizzards, please."

"Three long dogs!" shouted the man toward the kitchen. "All dressed up!" He turned and began to make the blizzards.

For the second time that day I began to think about home. I wondered what Kim was doing, if David made up with his stupid girlfriend, if Dad would grill steaks out, or if . . .

"Hey! Do you want to pay for this or just let the blizzards melt?" demanded a rough voice.

"Here you go," I mumbled. I was so embarrassed. He probably thought I was a dumb jerk. I handed him the money and picked up the bag all in one sweep. I started to turn and stopped myself. Wait for the change—gee, I just couldn't do anything right this afternoon.

"Seven-fifty, eight, nine, and ten," the man counted as he placed the two quarters and two ones in my hand. "Have a good day now."

I handed the change to Uncle Ron as I got into the car. I shifted the large bag to my right hand and then on my lap to try to hold it steady as he pulled onto the highway.

"You hungry?" he asked.

"Starved. I don't like airplane food. I hope Chelsea likes her blizzard."

"We'll soon find out," said Uncle Ron, as the car dropped down a steep hill and turned toward the parking area. He traveled slowly along the gravel road and parked under a maple tree.

As we got out of the car, I asked, "Do you want me to go in and look for Chelsea? I know I can find her, even if it is crowded."

"Gin-n-n-y-y-y! Gin-n-n-y-y-y!" a familiar voice rang out.

I turned to see Chelsea waving and running toward me. She looked more tan than usual and her thick brown hair was pulled back away from her face.

"I've been watching for you guys," she panted, as she gave me a bear hug. "Dad promised he would bring you over as soon as you got here. Food! Gee, Dad, you think of everything! Ginny, you look great. How was the trip? Have you been to Grandma's yet? I get to stay there, too. Who put slaw on these hot dogs?"

I never realized until now how much Chelsea was like her mom. I waited for a chance to speak. "I had them put on the slaw; that's what you ordered the last time we went to Frank's Dairy Bar. The trip was all right. Tell me more about staying at Grandma's."

"This was Mom and Dad's idea. Since your mom was going to be helping Grandma clean out the house and get it ready to sell, I was going

7

to keep you company. We have to do our part, too, helping them clean out and pitching the junk away. But at least I would be there, and we don't have to work all the time."

"Why? Is Grandma selling the house? Is she going to move? No one said anything to me about working. Gee, I'm glad you will be there." I sighed. "Is there anything else I need to know?"

"That's all I know," Chelsea said, between big bites of food. "But it will be fun. Grandma said we can keep some of her antiques and any of the junk from the coal bin."

"The coal what?" I asked.

"Coal bin. B-I-N. You know, it's like a little room in a basement or under a porch where you store coal," she explained.

"No, I don't know. We don't have a room like that in our house."

Seeing the look of confusion on my face, Chelsea continued, "We don't either, because we have electric heat. But Grandma and Grandpa at one time heated their house with a furnace, and had to shovel coal into the furnace. Nobody liked to go outside during the winter and bring in coal, so you had trucks dump it under your porch or in a basement room. You sunny California people don't know of such things," she teased.

"I still don't get it," I said. "Why are you so happy that we get to clean out a dirty coal bin?"

"Because," she leaned toward me and spoke in a mysterious voice, "this room has not been used as a coal bin for ages. Grandpa hid a lot of his special antiques and souvenirs there. I know we'll find some really neat stuff. We might even become rich."

I laughed and shook my head. "Oh, Chelsea, now I know why you are my favorite cousin. Who else would get excited about a dirty job like that? Coal bins and mountaineers . . . what a vacation!"

"Bite your tongue!" Chelsea shrieked as she threw an empty blizzard cup by my head. "We'll see who is dumb when I find valuable antiques. I might just keep them for myself."

"I doubt if any of us become rich and famous after being in the coal bin," said Uncle Ron. "You girls do need to help get the house ready to sell, and that is as good a room as any to start with. Let's pick up our mess and head for home."

We cleaned up around the table and started for the car. Three girls began calling for Chelsea from the pool area. She waved to her friends and climbed into the back seat next to me.

"I'm just glad you're here," she said. "It will be a good summer. You just wait and see."

Facts

1. Many Indian names label West Virginia towns, counties, rivers, and mountains.
2. Gen. Charles (Chuck) Yeager, born in Hamlin, West Virginia, was the first person to fly faster than the speed of sound. He broke the sound barrier in 1947 when he flew 750 miles (1206.75 kilometers) per hour. General Yeager served as pilot of Air Force I under President Nixon and as grand marshall of the inaguaral parade for President Bush.
3. West Virginia's Capitol, erected in 1931, was designed by Cass Gilbert. The gold-leafed dome is five feet seven and one-half inches higher than the United States Capitol.

West Virginia's Capitol complete with gold-leafed dome, was completed in 1931.

Chapter 2

The Old Trunk

"So this is a coal bin?" I asked.

"A coal bin. Isn't it neat?" Chelsea exclaimed.

"To be honest, Chelsea, I can't see why you are in such a hurry to dig into this mess." I stood in the narrow doorway surveying the small room.

"Just hand me the light and let's get started," Chelsea said.

"Come on, I just got here today, and now you want to start on this tonight. Can't it wait until morning?"

"What you don't understand, Miss California, is that I have been waiting for three weeks for you to get here," snapped Chelsea. "I'm sorry, Ginny. You're right, we'll wait until tomorrow. Who needs to see what's in the trunk anyway?"

"I can't even see a trunk. Hand me the light." I held the campfire battery lamp above my head and strained my eyes to find the trunk Chelsea was talking about. The room was about eight feet high and only four feet wide. It seemed to be ten feet long. It reminded me of the narrow *walk-in* closet in Mom and Dad's bedroom back home, except the closet had a light in the middle of it.

"What's that?" I asked, directing the beam of light to a black iron plate on the outside wall.

"That's the opening for the coal chute." Chelsea saw the look of confusion on my face. "It would take too long to shovel a ton of coal into a bucket and carry it into a house, so a chute would be placed from the back of the truck to this open hole at the top of the bin. Then a conveyer belt moved the coal from the truck to fill up the bin. That's why the opening is on the outside wall and near the top of the bin. Get it?"

"Hey, could a person crawl through that opening?" I asked.

"Only if he is skinny as a rail and someone in the house is dumb enough not to latch the iron door from the inside," Chelsea said reassuringly. "But that hatch has been sealed for years. Grandpa and Grandma switched to electric heat when Gramps retired."

"You know, it would be easier to store things with a light," I said. "I wonder why Grandpa didn't put one in?"

"Well, cuz, why don't you ask him that the next time you see him?" laughed Chelsea.

"You're awful. Is that why we get along so well?" I asked.

"Let's at least pull the trunk out tonight, okay? The rest can wait, but I would love to get into the trunk. It belonged to our great-great uncle. Anything in it would be at least a hundred years old or even older. How about it? I know we can get to it."

"Okay, you're on," I agreed, "but only the trunk. Do you want to hold the light or climb?"

"I'd better climb," Chelsea offered. "Remember, you're company, and if anything happens to you, it will be my fault. Hold that light over to the left. I need to move some things to get to the trunk. Can you see it? It's behind that huge crock and bird cage, back in the corner."

I moved the light over to the left and raised it above my head. Squinting my eyes I could make out something that looked like a large box behind a wooden bird cage. There were a lot of spider webs in that dim corner, and I was secretly glad I was "company" and didn't have to climb.

I wondered aloud, "How did you ever spot that thing, Chelsea?"

"I didn't," she answered, "Brad did. A couple of years ago Brad and I tried to get it out. He got to the corner and tried to move it. It seemed to be stuck. He gave it a hard yank and it came loose. So did Brad. Do you remember the summer you visited, and he had a broken ankle?"

"Wait a minute," I warned. "If you could get hurt, you'd better stop. Chelsea, I don't like this idea."

"The trunk is loose now. I'm not going to get hurt. If you'll just keep that lamp high, this will be a piece of cake," said Chelsea.

"If it's such a piece of cake, why didn't Brad go back and finish the job?" I questioned.

"He doesn't like cake!" laughed Chelsea, as she cautiously moved

12

over boxes and a roll of old carpet. "Here, hold this." She handed me the wooden bird cage.

"What kind of a bird lived in this cage?" I asked as I examined the thin wooden slats of the small square cage.

"Canaries," answered Chelsea. She moved a box marked CHRIST-MAS DECORATIONS toward the bottom of the heap and then stepped on top of it. The sound of crushing glass caused her to pause. "Uh-oh, bad move. Oh, well, Grandma could use some new ornaments."

I was still baffled about the small wooden cage. I asked, "Why would Grandpa and Grandma keep canaries in such small cages? How could any bird sing cooped up like that?"

"Oh, save me from California," chuckled Chelsea. "Don't you know anything about coal mining?"

"No," I answered indignantly. "We are civilized in the Golden State."

"Lighten up, Ginny. I'm just teasing," Chelsea said. "There is a lot of gas in a coal mine. A canary can smell it before a human being. So miners carried at least one canary with them on each shift. If the bird stopped singing, or became listless, they got out of there in a hurry."

"Oh," I replied. "I guess there are lots of things . . . Watch out!"

An old wagon that formed the base of Chelsea's box-piled ladder moved about three inches forward. It stopped abruptly, and she reached for the trunk in front of her. The boxes swayed under her feet as she held fast to the trunk.

"Are you okay?" I asked.

We heard footsteps overhead and the basement door opened. A beam of light and the sound of voices filtered down the long basement stairs.

"Chelsea, Ginny, are you girls all right?" Aunt Fran called.

"Tell her it's okay," whispered Chelsea.

"Nothing's wrong," I called back. "We're fine."

"Are you sure?" Aunt Fran asked.

I tried to sound confident when I answered, "Everything is okay."

"I'll let you girls know the minute Brad gets home. He should be here just any time now," said Aunt Fran.

She closed the door. We counted her footsteps as she moved down the hall, around the corner and into the kitchen.

I realized I had been holding my breath for the last two minutes. I asked, "Chelsea, can you get down from there? Should I move this old bicycle over for you to step on?"

"I got it! This time I really have it! The trunk . . . it's ours," Chelsea exclaimed.

"Forget the trunk, can you get down from there?"

"Piece of cake, remember?" she answered. "Just move the bicycle over here toward my foot, let me hand the trunk down to you, and then I will step down."

"I can't move anything until I set this lamp down," I said. I placed the lamp on the floor and moved the bike toward Chelsea's foot. When I looked up toward her, all I could see was the large trunk hovering over my head.

"Hurry," Chelsea said. "Get this thing. It's heavy."

"Just be careful," I pleaded. "If anything happens now our moms will really be mad."

I felt the heavy trunk move against my hands and into my arms. Something sharp seemed to be scraping against the inside of my right arm but I didn't dare move. Finally, the entire weight of the trunk was dropped. I didn't expect it to be so heavy. I let it slide onto the concrete basement floor using my fingers as a cushion. With one muted thud, it was on the ground.

"Trunk safe?" asked Chelsea.

"Trunk is safe. Now will you get down?"

"You bet. I can hardly wait to see what is inside," Chelsea said, as she moved from a swaying box to the bicycle and down to the floor. "Now whatever is in the trunk we share equally. Wait, I forgot Brad. We'll split three ways. Remember, he was the first to try and get this thing down."

"That's fine with me." I didn't expect any great treasures to be in the dusty old trunk.

"There's no lock," Chelsea said as she examined the trunk. "Hand me a rag and I'll get the dust off."

I handed her what looked to be an old high school sweater from the box nearest the lamp. She began brushing dust and cobwebs off the top of the trunk. My nose began to itch, and I sneezed three times.

"Look!" exclaimed Chelsea. "I've found a way to open it!" Two heavy leather straps lay across the top and buckled securely in the front. She pulled at one strap, but it wouldn't move.

"They buckle, just like a belt," I said. "Just slide the leather strap under the first part of the buckle and lift it up. It's no big deal, Chelsea."

"I know that," Chelsea replied.

14

She slid the strap under the base of the buckle and pulled upward. The brad did not release the buckle. Then she yanked the strap upward, and the leather tore apart like an old newspaper.

"Great," she moaned. "Now what?"

"Do you have a knife? The strap is old; nobody will be using the trunk. We'll cut it," I suggested.

"We'll need to go upstairs and . . . " Chelsea began. She paused when the door at the top of the stairs opened.

"Girls! Chelsea, Ginny! Chelsea, your brother's here," Aunt Fran called from the top of the basement stairs.

"It's Brad! Let's go," Chelsea shouted.

Chelsea threw the sweater on the floor and grabbed the lamp all in one sweeping motion. She leaped in front of me, ran out of the coal bin, and had one foot on the bottom step when she stopped. "Aren't you coming?" she asked.

"Sure," I answered. I started up the stairs behind Chelsea, my heart pounding. I knew Brad was only my cousin, but I really liked him. He didn't treat me like a sister or a cousin. He treated me like a girl, a special girl, and I liked that. I wish Mom would let me wear lipstick or eye makeup; then I would look older.

"Hey, Sis!" said Brad, giving Chelsea a big bear hug. "Miss me this week?"

"No way!" lied Chelsea. "We got the . . . "

"Ginny, you look great. I guess it's true; all California girls must be blonde and beautiful," remarked Brad as he put his arm around my shoulder and kissed me on the cheek.

All I did was laugh. I couldn't say anything. I had gone over and over in my mind the questions I would ask and the sophisticated comments I would make, but nothing came out of my mouth.

"We got the trunk," Chelsea said excitedly. "Brad, it's down, but it has two leather straps, and I was trying to open one, and it broke, and we were . . . "

"Wait a minute, wait a minute," Brad interrupted, "let me say hello to Grandma and Aunt Carol and then tell me about this trunk."

"But, Brad," Chelsea insisted, "it's the old brown one. The one you were trying to get when you broke your ankle. We've got it. You know, we thought there might be something valuable in it. Don't you remember?"

15

"Yes, I do. But your great treasure will just have to wait, Sis. Give me a minute and then I'll help you," Brad said in an adult tone.

"Yeah, sure," Chelsea replied, " 'Just give me a minute,' so I can forget about my dumb little sister. She's not important. She just risked her neck to get the trunk down *and* made Ginny promise to split any money or treasure three ways to include her big shot brother. 'Just give me a . . . ' "

"Chelsea, don't start that," snapped Aunt Fran. "Your brother just came through the door and already you two are bickering."

I was beginning to get homesick. This scene reminded me of my brother. I wondered if he would care about an old, dirty trunk.

"Hold it. Brad, you visit with your mother, Aunt Carol, and Grandmother. Ginny, Chelsea, can I help you girls with whatever trunk you keep talking about?" Uncle Ron asked.

"Yes!" Chelsea shouted. "And, Dad, we'll split the treasure with you."

Uncle Ron grinned and answered, "I don't expect a reward, just peace and quiet, thank you."

Chelsea shot out of the room and toward the basement stairs. Uncle Ron stepped back to let me in front of him, and we started downstairs toward the coal bin.

"Oh, Dad, I forgot," said Chelsea. "we need a knife to cut the leather straps. One of them broke. I didn't mean to break it."

"No problem," Uncle Ron assured her. "I have my pocketknife with me."

Uncle Ron picked up the camp light we had left on the floor. He held it above his head and surveyed the coal bin. He looked at the trunk and then into the far corner. He looked back at the trunk. He raised his eyebrows. "How did you girls get that trunk down?" he asked.

I figured it was time I opened my mouth. I couldn't let Chelsea take all the blame. "It was really easy, Uncle Ron. I climbed on the boxes and Chelsea held them real still. And it wasn't heavy, honest. We just set it right here on the floor."

"I have a hard time buying that," Uncle Ron said. "But it's here and you two are okay. I'll cut the straps but the two of you must promise me something."

Simultaneously Chelsea and I answered, "We promise. We won't ask you to do anything else."

"That's not it. Promise the two of you won't do any more dangerous

16

climbing. Now I know, you girls are going to be responsible for this room, but let Brad lift the things down. You can get into the trunk tonight, but that's it. You don't touch anything else until tomorrow or even later. Understand?''

"Yes, sir," I answered politely, lowering my head. I didn't want Uncle Ron upset with me.

"It's a deal," Chelsea answered nonchalantly.

Uncle Ron knelt and cut both leather straps in a matter of seconds. He tugged on the hasp, but nothing happened. "Chelsea," he said, "hand me that sweater on the floor, and you girls step back.''

He wrapped the sleeve around the hasp and stood up. He gave a firm jerk and the lid popped open. Dust flew everywhere.

I grabbed the light and moved to Uncle Ron's right side. Chelsea moved in on the left and just gazed in silence. Uncle Ron raised the top of the trunk completely and let it come to rest on a stack of boxes. He stepped back slowly, as Chelsea and I pushed forward.

"Just rags," whispered a disappointed Chelsea. "Now who in the world would save rags?''

"These aren't rags. They're clothes of some kind," I said, as I set the lamp back on the floor. I picked up a yellowing piece of cloth from the right hand side of the trunk and began to unfold it. "Look, Chelsea, it's a baby's dress. It's really long; it must have been a christening gown.'' I lifted it away from the trunk and the train fell almost to the floor.

Chelsea began to look more closely at the articles of clothing on her side of the trunk. "Do you think the whole thing is filled with baby clothes?" she asked.

"Tell you what," Uncle Ron said. "I'll move the trunk upstairs where you will have better light, and then you can go through it. Besides, I'm sure your grandmother can tell you who these things belonged to. How about it?''

I nodded and Chelsea stood there with her mouth gaping open. I had never seen her so depressed. I folded the gown, returned it to the trunk, and helped Uncle Ron lower the lid. Without anyone saying a word, Uncle Ron lifted the trunk onto his shoulder and started up the basement stairs. I pushed Chelsea, who appeared to be in a stupor, behind him.

"Coming through!" Uncle Ron shouted as he entered the narrow hallway, rounded the corner, and passed into the kitchen. He placed the trunk in the middle of the kitchen floor.

17

Brad, Grandma, Aunt Fran, and Mom grew silent. The four of them, seated around the oak table in the breakfast nook, just stared at the trunk in the middle of the floor.

"Ron," began Aunt Fran, "I'm sure your mother doesn't want that smelly, dirty trunk in the middle of her kitchen."

"The girls wanted to go through it, and I thought Mom could tell them about some of the things in the trunk." Then turning to Grandma, he said, "But, Mom, if you want I will . . . ."

"Leave it be," Grandma interrupted. They can pull out anything they want. I'll tell them what I know, but it won't be much. That trunk belonged to your father's Great-Uncle Joshua. Poor old Josh never settled down. He liked to drink a mite, maybe that's why he never married. He left the trunk at the old home place. When it was sold, your father just brought it here. Why, we never opened it. Your Dad always thought his Great-Uncle Joshua would come back for it. He never did.

"If it belonged to Grandpa's great-uncle, how old would it be?" I asked.

Grandma paused and her brow wrinkled. "Let's see. Your grandpa was born in 1915, and his father was born in 1882. So a great-uncle would be another generation back. So I figure Joshua was born around the 1840s or early 1850s. I recollect the older folks telling stories about him and Stonewall Jackson during the Civil War.

"That would make the trunk anywhere from 100 to 150 years old." commented Brad.

"Lordy, I guess you're right," chuckled Grandma. "I do need some help with my housecleanin'."

Aunt Fran and Mom left the table to examine the trunk. Uncle Ron raised the heavy lid, and this time he lowered the top all the way to the floor. The back hinges creaked a little and more dust escaped. A musty smell filled the air, and my nose began to itch. I could make out a child's knitted sweater and cap. A small, crib-size quilt filled the top along with the gown. The christening gown didn't look as yellow under the kitchen light as Mom lifted it from the trunk.

"Isn't this lovely," Mom commented. "I wonder who it belonged to or how many children wore this very gown."

"There are more baby clothes on this side," said Aunt Fran as she carefully removed articles of clothing from the trunk and onto a chair. "Help me lift off this open drawer, Ron, I want to see what's underneath."

18

Chelsea finally re-entered the twentieth century. She moved toward the trunk and a gleam came back to her eyes. "What drawer?" she asked.

Uncle Ron lifted out a rectangular compartment that appeared to be about eight inches deep. "All trunks have removable compartments that stack," he said. "That way certain things aren't mashed or ruined."

"All right!" Chelsea shouted. "Now let's get to the good stuff. What do you see?"

I moved next to Chelsea. We knelt in front of the trunk. Mom and Aunt Fran were on either side. Uncle Ron placed a second removable compartment containing clothes on the floor. Grandma and Brad peered over Chelsea and me, as we stared at two tattered books, some rolls of parchment paper, and a small square wooden box.

Chelsea reached for the top book. It appeared to be about eight inches long and six inches wide, with a worn brown leather cover. It was thicker and heavier than she imagined, because she needed both hands to lift it out. She opened the cover and studied the handwriting at the top of the page. It was faded and smeared as if it had been wet at one time. No one could read the name or the date. She turned another page and realized it was a diary. The dates and writing were clearer on these pages—'May 2, 1818 traveled to Wheeling, Virginia to sell horses to travelers crossing the National Road.' She handed this book to Grandma and reached for the smaller one. She opened the front cover and it came loose in her hands. The title page revealed the two words 'Holy Bible.' There was no visible name and as she turned the pages they fell from the binding.

"Better hand that to your mom for safekeeping," Uncle Ron suggested.

Chelsea handed the worn Bible to Aunt Fran. She passed out the remaining rolls of parchment to Mom and Brad. "Here," she said, putting the small wooden box in my hands, "you open this one."

The wooden box was about two inches square. I felt something shift inside when Chelsea handed it to me, so I knew it wasn't empty. I lifted the lid and help my breath. A soft piece of linen was wrapped round a small, but heavy object. I lifted the cloth and its contents from the box and placed them on the floor. I unfolded the first layer and caught a glimpse of something shiny. I hurriedly removed the second layer and gasped.

"Are those diamonds?" I asked. "What are the red ones? Do you think . . . "

"We're rich! We're rich! I knew it! I knew we'd find a treasure!" Chelsea shouted gleefully as everyone crowded around.

I was still confused. "But I'm not sure what this is. It's a little too big and heavy for a brooch. Mom, are these *REAL* diamonds?" I asked.

A glazed look came over Aunt Fran's face as she gently pushed me aside for a closer look at the jeweled ornament. "Ron, you don't think . . . No, it couldn't be. . . . Well, I'm not sure . . . "

"You're not sure about what?" Uncle Ron asked.

"A golden horseshoe. It's a golden horseshoe!" Aunt Fran exclaimed. "I can't believe it. Did you know, Alex. . . . "

"It's shaped like a horseshoe, but it is too small to be a real horseshoe," Mom said as she turned it over in her hands.

"Is it gold? Is it real? What do you think we can get for it?" asked Chelsea, bouncing up and down.

"If this is what I think it is, it belongs in a museum. It's a part of history," Aunt Fran remarked. "Did you know . . . "

Chelsea shouted, "Sold! To the museum that offers the best price!"

"Oh, no, you couldn't do that," began Aunt Fran. "This might be a valuable part of West Virginia's history and it won't be for sale, young lady."

"But, Mom, finders keepers, remember?" Chelsea insisted.

"Now just calm down, you two," said Uncle Ron. "Fran, what do you know about this golden horseshoe?"

"It could be very valuable. It would be a least two hundred years old," said Aunt Fran as her voice shifted into that schoolteacher tone. "Alexander Spotswood was lieutenant governor of Virginia in the early 1700s. He was interested in the western expansion of the colony, so he led a group of explorers into the Shenandoah Valley. He was a wealthy gentleman, so this expedition was like a grand picnic. The group included about sixty men, thirty gentlemen, many servants, and four Indian guides. The gentlemen wore their fancy clothes, you know, the lacy shirts, silk vests, and velvet waist coats. They traveled with fine linen, silver, the best food possible, and lots of wine and spirits. Each night when they camped, a fancy meal would be served, the gentlemen would dine in style, and then drink a toast to good King George. Everytime they crossed a mountain or large river, they would name it after the king, drink a toast to his health, and fire a volley of shots."

"Mom," interrupted Brad as he rolled his eyes, "a gold horseshoe, remember?"

Aunt Fran gave Brad her stern schoolteacher look. "I'm getting to that part. When the group returned to Jamestown, Alexander Spotswood gave each of the gentlemen a miniature golden horseshoe, and they formed a special group, the Knights of the Golden Horseshoe. If that is an original horseshoe, it would have a Latin inscription on the back. 'Sic Juvat Transcendere Montes.' That means 'Thus it was decided to cross the mountains.' "

"That's what it says," Mom remarked. "Now what do we do with this piece of history?"

"Nothing tonight," said Uncle Ron. "This has been one long day. It's 12:30 A.M. Carol, do you realize you and Ginny have been up for twenty-eight hours? We'll put the horseshoe in the toolbox under the kitchen sink until morning. Tomorrow, after everyone has had a good night's sleep, I'll call Charleston. Maybe someone at the West Virginia Museum and Cultural Center can tell us about the horseshoe."

"But, Dad." Chelsea moaned, "we found . . . "

Uncle Ron stated, "Tomorrow. Now that's it. Let's go to bed."

Good-nights were said and the adults began directing Brad, Chelsea, and me to bedrooms. We had the usual orders to shower, brush our teeth, and go promptly to sleep. Chelsea and I merely exchanged glances and smiled.

Facts

1. Canaries were used to detect gas in early coal mining history.
2. Lt. Alexander Spotswood did lead an expedition through the Appalachian Mountains around June 20, 1716. A miniature fourteen-carat golden horseshoe was distributed to each of the thirty gentlemen after the expedition. Six of the horseshoes were encrusted with genuine jewels, six diamonds, and five sapphires. The Smithsonian Institute in Washington, D.C., placed a monetary value of an original jewel-encrusted horseshoe at one hundred thousand dollars and its historical value at five hundred thousand dollars.
3. The tradition of the pin inspired the Golden Horseshoe Ceremony at which top eighth-grade West Virginia History students are knighted and presented with replicas of the original horseshoe.

Chapter 3

The Mound Builders

"Ginny, Ginny, you awake?" Chelsea whispered. "Come on, sleepy head, it's 9:30 in the morning. You're not much fun when it comes to late night talks, you know?"

"I'm sorry," I answered. "I remember you saying something last night about selling the golden horseshoe and . . . I guess I just dozed off."

"Dozed off, dozed off," teased Chelsea, "it was more like the sleep of the dead. But I knew you weren't dead, you know why?"

"Why?" I asked.

"You snored!" laughed Chelsea. "Honest, you did."

"No, I didn't. I have never snored," I answered sharply.

Grandma called from the kitchen, "This kitchen closes in five minutes, anyone wanting to eat had better shake a leg."

"Hurry, move it." Chelsea leaped from her twin bed. "This is the only place I know where I can get fresh blueberry muffins." She stepped into her jeans, slipped on her sandals, and was pulling a blue and gold West Virginia University sweat shirt over her head as she started out the doorway.

I jumped from my bed and slid on a pair of jeans, my Grateful Dead T-shirt, and my new Reeboks. Mom had insisted I get new tennis shoes before our trip. Chelsea was two steps ahead of me going into the breakfast room.

"Milk?" Chelsea asked me as she headed for the refrigerator door.

"That's fine." I nodded. I reached for two glasses from the cabinet above the dishwasher.

The timing was perfect. Grandma put a dozen steaming blueberry muffins on the table just as I sat down and Chelsea poured the milk. Chelsea and I reached for the muffins at the same time. She immediately spread butter over the top of her muffin and bit it in half.

A smile crossed her face, and she closed her eyes. "Grandma," said Chelsea, "nothing could be better than this."

Remembering all the lectures from Mom, I cut my muffin in half, buttered only one side, and took a dainty bite. "She's right, Grandma; this is the best muffin I've ever eaten."

"Did I hear the word 'muffin,' coupled with 'blueberry'?" asked Brad, bouncing into the kitchen. "I know you made these just for me, because you like me best." Brad reached for two muffins and took Chelsea's glass of milk.

"Hey!" yelled Chelsea. "Get your own milk, and she does not like you best. Blueberry muffins are my favorites."

Grandma beamed. "I'm sure there is enough to go around. If not, I'll make more. Brad, get your own milk and give Chelsea hers."

"You're right, Grandma," said Brad, handing Chelsea her glass of milk. "You just never know when you might pick up rabies." Brad got up and walked toward the kitchen sink. "Anyone check the famous horseshoe this morning?"

Grandma answered, "Your mother called the director at the museum in Charleston this morning. I think her name was White or Whitten. She asked lots of questions and said she wanted to see it . . . "

"They didn't take it to her, did they?" Brad asked as he looked for the toolbox.

"Oh my, no," she answered. "It should be right there."

"It is," sighed Brad, as he turned toward us holding the horseshoe. He brought the horseshoe to the table and put it in the center for all of us to see.

It was really beautiful. I didn't get to study it last night, and I missed some of its details. There were eleven alternating stones, five red ones, and six clear ones. It was probably pure gold, because niches were visible in the soft metal at both ends.

"Do you think those are real diamonds?" I asked, as I picked up the horseshoe and turned it over in my hand.

"You can't tell until we clean it up and have it appraised," Grandma said. "I don't think we'd be hurtin' it any if we polished it up a bit before that director gets here. Brad, fetch me the polish I use on the silver. It's in the cupboard next to the back door."

Chelsea offered, "I'll get some rags."

I turned the horseshoe back and forth in my hand. It picked up the sunlight from the one breakfast nook window. The gleam from the lower stone was dazzling. It grew larger and brighter. All I could see was a huge ball of blazing light. Suddenly, everything around me became dark and still. *Nothing*—a silent, blank video screen. I was terrified. My mind kept telling me to yell, but I couldn't utter a sound. My eyes kept straining to see, but total darkness surrounded me. I recognized a faint voice. It was Brad's, yet he sounded so far away. I saw something flash. A red and white light was swirling at the far end of a tunnel. It came closer and grew larger. It was a huge golden horseshoe with sapphires and diamonds spinning faster and faster above my head. I reached up, I had to stop it. I grabbed hold of one end. It wouldn't stop, it kept spinning. My hand was burning, but I couldn't let go.

"Stop! S–t–o–p it!!" I screamed with a strange voice that seemed to be outside my body. "Help! Make it stop!"

"Ginny, Ginny, you're okay," Chelsea's reassuring voice echoed in my ears.

"Come on, over here," Brad's voice called from somewhere in the distance.

Chelsea's voice trembled. "Ginny, give me your hand, I think Brad found a way out of here."

"All I can see is that golden horseshoe with its bright lights," I responded. "I don't feel so good, Chelsea; my head aches. I'm dizzy. I think it's that brilliant glow. It hurts to look at it."

"That's where we're going, toward that light. It's not a horseshoe, Ginny, it's an opening to this cave," Chelsea remarked as she pulled me along with her.

"A cave," I gasped. "What do you mean . . . a cave?"

"We're in a cave and I want out of here," said Chelsea. "That's all I know. Now come on. Brad is up ahead."

We held tightly to each other, as we moved toward the light. Water squished in my tennis shoes. I reached to the left and felt rocks, some smooth and some jagged. Something screeched and flew above my head.

"Chelsea, there is something in here besides us," I whispered.

Chelsea just squeezed my right arm tighter and quickened her steps. "Come on, we're almost there," she said.

Brad was clearly visible now as he stepped into the mouth of the grotto. He reached for Chelsea and me and led us out into the bright sunlight. We stood in a small clearing in front of the cave looking down into a lush, vine-covered valley. Broad-leafed plants, taller than me, with red or green and white striped leaves, formed a canopy over the ground. Mountains, thickly forested by tall trees with glossy leaves, loomed behind us.

"Where in the world are we?" I asked, holding my head.

"I'm not sure," Brad said, "I've never seen anything like this, but we'll find our way out, trust me."

"This can't be, no way," Chelsea insisted. "What's the joke? Now we were all eating blueberry muffins; come on, you guys. I don't want to play this game any longer. What gives?"

"Well, I'm not certain. It's all so weird. But I have a theory," said Brad scratching his head. "I know this sounds crazy, but it has to do with time and dimen . . . "

"Listen, hear that?" I asked.

"Get back in the cave," Brad said, "and don't make a sound."

We scurried into the cave and pressed our bodies against its side. Brad motioned for Chelsea and me to get down. We squatted down to the floor. I could feel water dripping on my back and mud oozing under my feet. My heart was pounding so loudly that it echoed in my ears.

"Aaeeii, aeeii!" came the shout.

I could hear human voices, several speaking at once, but I couldn't understand what they were saying. The voices, intermingled with grunts, came closer.

Brad stooped low and backed into the cave with us.

Passing the entrance of the cave were five shaggy-haired men. They weren't very tall, just about my height. Their bodies were very hairy; they even had hair matted on their shoulders. Animal skins were tied around their waists and hung in scallops to their knees. Each one carried a crude looking weapon with a point made of a vee-shaped black rock tied to a sapling with a strip of leather.

The man in front, leading the group, held an animal tusk about eight inches long in his left hand. He held it like a knife and raised it above his head as he called, "Aaeeii–i–!"

The men answered in grunts as they followed their leader in single file past the cave.

The last two men in the group carried a large tusked pig that was hanging from a tree branch they balanced on their shoulders. They struggled under its weight as their bare feet dug into the rich, black soil on the mountain slope.

I listened as the voices moved off in the distance. "Brad, what did you mean about time?" I finally asked.

Brad, with a grim face, said, "I'm not real sure about this, but if it isn't a bad dream, I think we've been sent back in time."

Chelsea moaned. "Oh great. I needed this trip."

My cousin was older, but sometimes she acted like a pouting brat. "What can we do? How do we get back to Grandma's?" I asked.

"I don't know, Gin," Brad answered, "I don't even know how we got here in the first place. Let's move outside and look around."

We left the cave. Once outside, we surveyed the entrance and decided this would be our home base until we figured out how to leave.

"Do you think those men we saw earlier could help us? I know we don't speak their language, but do you think we could use sign language to get them to understand?" I asked.

"Let's not try that right away. That was a hunting party. They had killed a wild boar, so I guess they aren't cannibals. But, I'm not so sure we would be safe with them. Let's look around first, before we contact anyone," Brad said.

"I think we'd better stick together from now on," Chelsea said.

"Good idea, Sis," Brad said. He led the way up the mountain. Away from the cave the foliage became thicker. At times we were unable to see the sky, only thick green leaves above us and moist, loose soil under our feet. We finally reached the mountaintop and looked into another valley.

An oval stone stockade, about four miles long, encircled a village. Huts, crudely constructed of small trees tied together with strips of leather and roofs of dried, woven long grass, bordered the stone wall. They looked like something from the TV show "Gilligan's Island." Small garden plots dotted all of the enclosed area except the very center which was dominated by two earthenwork mounds, each taller than a two-story house. The mounds were located on either side of a flat ceremonial area about the size of basketball court. Approximately seventy-five individuals were moving freely within the enclosed area. Women and children were working in the gardens, while some men were moving clay pots toward the center ceremonial area. The hunting party was just entering the village. Everbody stopped what they were doing to greet the returning hunters. Shouts, grunts, and some low chanting could be heard as the joyous group began a swaying, dancing movement. The hunters joined in the chanting and dancing with their escorts to the ceremonial area. All movement and noises stopped as the leader of the hunting party raised the animal tusk above his head.

He chanted, "Aaeeii, aaeeii, hukka, dalb. Hukka dalb mom tet. Hukka dalb mom tar cet hukka dable mom tea.

The inhabitants responded, "Tet mom tar mom tea."

The leader continued, "Ionit hukka dalb. Aaeeii!!"

The last scream caused the group to disband. Tribe members started toward the huts, as the hunting party began to gut and skin the boar. Two young men about Brad's age appeared. One carried wood and the other a flaming torch. They proceeded to dig a shallow pit and prepare a circle fire.

"Looks like we're just in time for dinner," said Brad. "Shall we go down for a closer look?"

We moved as quietly as possible toward the village with Brad leading the way. The tall grass and shrubs gave plenty of cover. As we came closer, we were unable to see over the wall, but the entrance was visible.

Brad whispered and signaled with his hand, "Keep down; they might have guards posted."

We were close enough to hear voices and smell the roasting meat. Chelsea sniffed deeply and remarked, "It didn't take long to start the barbecue. I prefer medium rare. Do you think they have enough for three more?"

"Shhh," scolded Brad. "This isn't a time to be funny, Chelsea. You two stay here. I'm going to go inside the wall. I'll signal you if it's safe for you to come. If anything should happen, go back to the cave, understand?"

I nodded. "Okay."

"Brad," Chelsea began, "be careful. And, eh, I'm sorry for some . . ."

"Save it, Sis," Brad replied. "We'll get out of here."

Brad stooped low and dashed to the outside of the wall. He pressed his body against the stone and peeped into the entrance. He glanced a second time and turned his head to the right and left. His third look was long and steady. He motioned for Chelsea and me to join him. When we reached the wall, he immediately put his index finger to his lips to signal us not to talk. He ducked inside the wall and to the right. Chelsea went

27

next, and I followed. We snuggled behind a hut straining our eyes and ears.

In front of the hut sat an old woman, Grandma's age, and two boys about three or four years old. The old woman had a pelt strapped around her waist, but the boys were naked. She was busy pounding an oval rock into a hollow tree trunk as the boys played with turtleshells. To the right of the hut was a garden plot about fifteen feet square. A younger woman was hoeing between rows of beans and squash. I held my breath when she stopped hoeing. She picked up a woven basket filled with squash and started toward the older female. The two women exchanged words. The older lady scooped the cornmeal that she had been grinding from inside the hollow trunk and put it into a basket. The crude hoe and rock pestle were placed inside the hut. Each woman picked up one of the boys and a basket filled with food and started toward the ceremonial area.

"The party must be over there," Chelsea pointed toward the center of the two large mounds, "and we weren't invited. So let's get out of here, Brad."

"Take it easy," Brad said, "and for heaven's sake keep your voice down."

"I'd like to know where we are and how we're going to get out of here?" I asked.

Brad said, "I think we are among mound builders, that's why I want to get a closer look at those manmade hills. These are definitely prehistoric Indians."

"Oh, no. It's coming back to me, Adena-Hopewell cultures. Where is Mom when you really need her?" Chelsea responded shaking her head. "We had this in West Virginia History class. These people lived more than five hundred years before Christ. Holy Cow! Brad, Ginny, we've got to get out of here."

"How?" Brad and I asked simultaneously.

"I don't know. Brad, you're the oldest; you think of something," Chelsea said.

"Look, this must have something to do with that stupid horseshoe. Ginny, where did you put it?" asked Brad.

"I-I-, I don't know. The last time I had it, we were at Grandma's," I answered as I searched my pockets. "Honest, I don't know where it is."

"Maybe we should go back and look for it," Chelsea suggested.

I snapped, "Where?"

28

"In the cave, Ginny. You were the last one to have it in your hand at Grandma's. So when we were sent on this great time trip you must have been holding it." Chelsea continued, "Let's look for it in the cave and then get out of here. This place gives me the creeps."

"Aaeii! Adem!" screamed a bushy-haired, stoop-shouldered man as he lifted his spear and pointed it at Brad's head.

I felt a sharp pang of fear; it was hard to breathe.

The yellow-skinned man came closer. I could see a glare in his oval eyes as he studied the three of us. His mouth gaped open, revealing sharp long buck teeth. His eyebrows formed a continuous line above his wide flat nose. His dark hair was matted and dirty.

He shouted a second time, "Aaeeii! Adem adem!"

His call was answered by shouts of, "Adem, ona tok! Adem!"

Three more prehistoric men appeared with raised spears and surrounded us. One short, stocky warrior with dirty hands reached to touch my hair. I backed away from him and fell against Chelsea, knocking her down. Brad helped her to her feet and tried to stand in front of us.

"Wait! Stop!" Brad shouted. "Who is in charge? We're not here to hurt anyone."

As the men grunted and spoke in their strange tongue, a woman appeared with a heavy grape vine. She proceeded to tie our hands and lead us in single file toward the center of the village. The villagers parted as we were ushered to the leader of the hunting party.

"Boodka dat tok," he spoke, looking first at Brad and then at me.

"Boodka dat tok," I answered with all the courage I could possibly muster. I had no idea what I had said.

"Logdo totam?" he questioned.

"Logda totam," I responded.

That wasn't the right answer. The Indians shouted and seemed disgruntled. Some of the women moved closer. I recognized the young woman with the hoe that we had seen earlier. She reached out and touched my hair. I tried not to flinch as she continued to finger my reddish blonde curls. She mumbled an invitation and two other women joined her. Hair seemed to be popular as they moved to feel Chelsea's thick brown locks and Brad's short hair. The group quieted down. We stood still and jerked away from no one.

The leader lifted the long animal tusk, barked out commands, and pointed toward one of the mounds. The woman who had tied our hands started toward us. Two Indians followed with their spears pointed at

Brad. She paused to light a torch, from the fire under the spitted pig, and then stopped in front of me. She checked to see if my hands were tied securely. She took hold of the vine rope and let us through a concealed entrance into the nearest mound.

The stench was awful. I thought I was going to throw up. Light flickering from the torch revealed a circular wall of tree trunks driven tightly together into the ground. The ceiling looked similar to the thatch on the huts outside. Rocks and many layers of dirt had been added to this framework to create the external appearance of a hill. I stumbled over some large pieces of pottery before I made out the ghastly sight on the dirt floor. It was a human body, a dead human body. That was the horrible odor I smelled. I wanted to cry out but nothing would come out of my mouth. I couldn't make a sound. I tried to look away, but she led the three of us right in front of the corpse. I glanced at Chelsea and Brad. Chelsea looked as white and ghastly as the rotting body. Brad's mouth dropped open as he shot a quick glance back at Chelsea.

Brad muttered, "Don't scream. Whatever you do, don't scream."

The woman placed the torch in a recess and left us without uttering a sound. The two guards followed her and positioned themselves outside the secluded entrance.

"I'm going to vomit," Chelsea said as she turned away from the corpse. "Forget dinner, the barbecue or anything to eat."

"Brad, what are we going to do?" I pleaded.

"Give me a minute; I'll think of something," Brad answered in a serious tone.

I stood, for what seemed like hours, waiting for my eyes to become accustomed to the dim light from the flickering torch. I took a long look at the figure on the floor. The body was completely covered with animal skins except for the arms. Three metal bracelets decorated the right upper arm and a band of long feathers was visible above the elbow on the left arm. A necklace of disk-shaped beads lay in three rows across the chest. A five inch pendant of ivory was hanging from the bottom tier. A wide strip of leather dotted with hazy blue stones formed a headband. The hands lay at the side of the body and each rested on a weapon. The left hand clasped a sharp, pointed tusk and the right held a spear. A tobacco pipe and a comb made of bone were placed near the head. Various pieces of bone and rock, probably tools, were lying near the right hand. A walking stick was placed under the feet.

30

"Can we sit down for a while, since we're not going to be rushing out of here?" moaned Chelsea.

"Not yet," Brad answered. "Ginny, lead us toward the corpse. See that wide piece of bone, the one near the right hand?"

"Yeah," I replied moving toward the body.

"If Chelsea can get that bone, it looks like it has a sharp edge on one side, one of us can get loose," Brad suggested.

By this time we had inched our way next to the corpse. Chelsea tried to stoop to reach the bone.

"We're tied together. Remember, you guys must bend down, too," said Chelsea.

I bent down and tried to give Chelsea room to reach for the sharp tool. I couldn't see her, but I could feel her movements behind me."

"Got it!" she exclaimed. "Now the hard part, how do we all stand up at the same time?"

"Up on the count of three," explained Brad. "And take it slow; if one of us falls, we all go down. One-two-three."

As I stood I could feel Chelsea also rise. Brad was the last on his feet. I turned as far as the rope allowed to try and watch Chelsea. She began moving the bone back and forth across the vine connecting her with Brad.

Brad urged, "Way to go, Sis. Come on. You can do it."

Simultaneously the vine broke, and Chelsea dropped the tool. "Oh no, now what?" she asked.

"I'm loose. I can pick it up." Brad continued, "I'll cut the vines holding your hands and then you can free Ginny and me."

Brad retrieved the tool from the floor and held it gingerly between his bound hands. He cut furiously at the vines holding Chelsea's hands until she was completely free.

Chelsea immediately untied Brad's hands and the two of them loosened the tangled tendrils that held me.

Brad ordered, "Pick up the vines; when they come back for us, spread them around your wrists. We can't let them know we're loose." He scanned the inside of the mound. "Let's move away from the torch and into the shadows. It will be harder for them to see us."

"Do you have a plan?" I asked.

"Not really," Brad replied. "The first chance we have to get out of here we will. Then I guess it's back to that cave. We've got to find the horseshoe."

31

The three of us settled away from the torch, against the circular wall. As I moved my back against the wooden frame, trying to get comfortable, I realized the back of my shirt was getting wet. I turned and tried to see where the moisture was coming from, but it was too dark. I felt with my hands and found a portion of the framework had split under the weight of the earth that had been piled on top. That's why the men were carrying clay pots toward the ceremonial grounds! They were trying to patch up the splintered wall with clay and dirt.

"Brad, Chelsea," I whispered excitedly, "over here, quick."

Chelsea and Brad moved quietly toward me.

I pointed to the broken splintered trees and pulled them effortlessly apart, "Look, all we have to do is dig our way out."

"Way to go, cuz," Chelsea said patting me on the back. "Let's get at it."

"Hold it," cautioned Brad. "We need a lookout. Remember, we're not alone."

"I'm your lookout," offered Chelsea.

"Okay, Ginny, let's dig," Brad said.

Brad and I got down on our knees and began to scoop the dirt away with cupped hands. As we moved the loose earth, the gap in the framework widened. Within minutes, a tunnel about three feet long and just wide enough for a person to slither through was ready for completion.

"My hand is through," I whispered to Brad.

"Make the hole just wide enough to see out," Brad replied.

"It's getting dark, I don't see any huts," I answered, as I shifted my position inside the tunnel. "Wait, there's the wall. We must be on the side of the mound."

"Great," said Brad without enthusiasm. "That means we'll be in the open at least fifty feet before we reach the wall. Then we'll need to circle half way around the village to get out. That's going to be some run."

"But it's our only . . . "

"Someone's c-c-coming!" sputtered Chelsea, as she hurried toward us.

"Grab the vines. Twist them around your wrists and pretend to be asleep," whispered Brad.

I grabbed my set of vines, twisted them furiously around my wrists, and huddled between Chelsea and Brad. Chelsea leaned her head on my shoulder, as I settled against Brad and shut my eyes tightly. A horrible

32

thought crossed my mind. When we were bound and led in, I was in front of Chelsea. What if they noticed? I could hear voices inside the mound, it was too late to move now.

"Uugha omph," spoke a voice a few feet away.

"Atha, ahta pha," said a voice just a few inches from my face.

I wanted to open my eyes, just to peep, but I was afraid to move. I felt a tug on the vine ropes. I could feel Brad shift beside me as his hands were being lifted.

"Nau ta, nau ta. Othi pha atha," remarked a commanding voice.

There was movement above me. Padded footsteps mingled with grunts signaled that the captors were leaving. I squinted enough to see the backs of three Indians as they moved toward the narrow entrance and left the mound. Brad sighed. Chelsea raised her head from my shoulder but remained silent.

Minutes passed before my heart slowed down and I had the courage to speak. "Do you think they'll be back?" I asked.

"I hope not," Brad continued. "At least not until morning. And if we're lucky, we'll be gone by then."

"Brad, I want to go home," whimpered Chelsea. "I've had enough of this time dimension stuff. I don't even want that stupid horseshoe. I don't want anything from that old trunk, not even treasure. The museum director can have it. All of it. In fact I . . . ."

"Hey, take it easy," Brad soothed. "We'll wait an hour or so and then we'll make a run for it. Just rest for now, okay?"

I agreed in my heart with Chelsea, but I didn't want my cousins to know how frightened I was. I tried to sound confident and mature when I said, "Nothing to it. We'll be out of here and back home in no time."

I leaned my head against the framework and closed my eyes. I realized how tired and hungry I was. I tried to picture the escape route. I knew we could find our way out of the camp, but I wasn't sure if we could find our way back to the cave. And then how would we find the horseshoe? What if the horseshoe had nothing to do with this trip back in time? This must just be a bad dream. Mom is going to wake me . . . .

"Ginny, it's time," Brad whispered. "I've finished the tunnel. Here is the plan. I'll go out first. When you see me signal, send Chelsea. You count to ten and follow Chelsea. If any one of us is caught, the other person is to keep going. Head for the cave. Got it?"

I nodded. Brad turned to go into the tunnel. The torch was almost out, but I could see Chelsea's pale face as she watched her brother leave.

33

I patted her hand before I moved into the tunnel to await Brad's signal. I strained my eyes for Indians as Brad dashed across the clearing and crouched against the wall. He motioned to send Chelsea. I backed out of the tunnel and made room for Chelsea to enter.

"It's clear; hurry," I said.

Chelsea crawled into the tunnel and I followed. She paused long enough to spot Brad and then she left.

Run faster, run faster, I thought as I started to count aloud. "One, two three," *I'm in a grave alone with a dead body,* my mind kept reminding me. "Four, five, six, seven . . . " I thought, *Forget this and leave.*

I ran as fast as I could across the clearing. As I approached, Brad started to move along the wall with Chelsea following about three feet back. I fell in behind Chelsea. My heart was beating so hard, it hurt to breathe. I tried to stop gasping. I was afraid the panting sounds would give us away as we passed the huts. I spied the entrance up ahead. Brad held up his hand for us to stop. Chelsea plowed into Brad and the two lay sprawled on the ground. No one moved. I listened and waited for an Indian to come out of a hut and discover us. I held my breath and tried to keep my trembling body still. No one appeared. Brad signaled for Chelsea and me to stay down while he struggled to his hands and knees. He crawled to the entrance and peered around the corner. Chelsea and I staggered to our knees. Instead of following behind, I crawled beside her toward the entrance and freedom. Once outside the wall, the three of us ran upright, but single file, along the path through the parted leaves. I felt wide leaves swish against my jeans as vines and then branches slapped my face and scratched my arms. After fifteen or twenty minutes of running, Brad slowed to a walk. We paused at the top of the mountain to look back at the village. There was still no movement in the valley below.

"We made it," I panted, hugging Chelsea.

Chelsea grinned and nodded. She reached to hug Brad.

"We're not home yet," he cautioned. "Sooner or later they'll come looking for us. We've got to find the horseshoe before they find us."

"Can't we rest, for just a minute?" pleaded Chelsea.

Brad replied in a stern voice, "No, Chelsea, not until we're safe at home."

"Let's go," I said, leading the way down the narrow path toward the cave. For some unknown reason I was familiar with every turn. I felt I had been here before.

Moving down the hill was much easier. We were able to slacken our pace and still cover a lot of ground. By dawn we stood in front of the cave.

"We'll start looking in the back section where we gained consciousness," Brad said.

"You mean you all were out, too?" I asked.

"Sure. Did you think we got here by plane?" Chelsea asked, sounding like her old self again.

"Did you see that huge spinning horseshoe? And those lights?" I asked.

"I didn't see anything," Brad said. "I just blinked my eyes and was in the back of a cave."

"Same with me," responded Chelsea. "I was looking at the horseshoe you were holding and bingo! The next thing I know I'm in the back of a dumb cave and you're complaining about a headache."

"I was looking at the same horsehoe, Ginny. It was in your hand, so you must have had it when we were flashed through time," Brad added.

As I started into the cave, I asked, "How do we find a miniature horseshoe in the dark without a flashlight?"

"We search with our hands," replied Brad. "Besides, it's not totally dark. Look up ahead."

Some scant beams of light seeped through several long, narrow cracks in the back of the cave. Water trickled through these same cracks and could be heard dripping in the distance. The grotto seemed to narrow and grow cooler as we groped our way toward the rays of light. My tennis shoes began to squish with mud, and I had to crouch to keep from hitting my head on the cave ceiling.

I saw a gleam in the distance, or was that just a beam of light? I forced my eyes to search the darkness for any glimmer of light. There it was! I know I saw it!

"Chelsea, Brad, over here! Follow me!" I yelled.

I hurried to the spot. The flash disappeared. I was standing in a puddle of water. I remarked sullenly, "I thought I saw something here. I guess it was the light reflecting on the water."

"Or something *under* the water!" Brad shouted. He shoved me aside, fell on his knees, and searched frantically in the puddle.

35

"You really think so?" I asked. I joined Brad in the underwater search. I moved both hands back and forth in the cold water, letting my fingers curve around hidden objects.

Chelsea shouted, "Wait! Something moved back there."

She pointed to the edge of the puddle near Brad's knee. Sure enough, half-submerged was the golden horseshoe.

I reached for the mystic horseshoe and picked it up ever so carefully. Water trickled down my arm when I held it up to the light. It was the same horseshoe; a few niches on both ends, five sapphires and . . . .

"Oh, no," My voice trembled, "a diamond is missing. What if it doesn't work. What if it won't take us home?"

"Let me see it," said Brad. "Ginny, turn it around to the light. I can't see it from here. Hold it up higher."

I turned toward Brad and held the horseshoe high above my head. I turned it from side to side in a thin beam of light, so Brad could see a diamond was missing. Then it started again—the darkness. A total blank. The horseshoe was way above my head spinning faster and faster. I couldn't stop it. I couldn't hold on to it any longer. I tried to yell, but I couldn't make a sound.

Facts

1. Prehistoric Indians lived in the area that is now West Virginia as early as 12,000 B.C.
2. Indians associated with the Adena-Hopewell cultures occupied the area one thousand years before the birth of Christ. They were called *Mound Builders,* because they built burial mounds for their dead. They practiced simple agriculture, lived in circular houses, made tools and weapons from flint, bones and shells.
3. Over three hundred mounds are visible in West Virginia today, along the Ohio river and in the Kanawha Valley.
4. The largest single (earthwork) mound east of the the Mississippi River is the Grave Creek Mound in Moundsville, West Virginia.
5. Archaeologists have found skeletons, copper bracelets, small beads, sea shells, pottery, tools, and weapons in West Virginia mounds.
6. Petroglyphs (rock carvings) by prehistoric Indians have been found in Harrison, Cabell, Monongalia, and Ohio counties.

Chapter 4

Blennerhassett Island

Faintly I cried out, "Help me! Brad, Chelsea, where are you?"

"We're here, Gin; it's okay. You're all right," responded Brad in a reassuring voice.

I tried to move but I was pinned between wooden enclosures. I realized my legs were bent and numb. My right arm was under my throbbing head. I thought of the horseshoe, that must be what I was clenching in my left hand. I struggled to open my eyes. The light was blinding.

I heard Chelsea moan. "Are we home yet?" she asked.

"Not unless we moved to an island. Chelsea, don't move like that! You're going to turn this boat over," Brad threatened.

I blinked my eyes open but closed them immediately. The sun directly overhead was blinding. I felt movement, rocking, like I was on my waterbed at home. That's what Chelsea meant; I must be lying on the bottom of a boat. I struggled to move my legs and sit up.

"Easy, Ginny," Chelsea's voice soothed, as she gently raised the upper part of my body. "Hold still; your legs are under the seat. You pull them up slowly while I guide them. Ready?"

"I'll loosen her legs," insisted Brad. "You stay on your end of the boat, Sis."

"All right, all right," Chelsea continued. "I'm just trying to be helpful."

When I felt pressure on my legs I tried to pull them toward me. That didn't work. I forced my eyes open, reached down with both hands, and pulled my numb legs upward. Gee, was I sore. The small rowboat rocked when I pulled. I grabbed for the sides to hold on.

37

"Did I hear you say 'island,' Brad?" I asked dumbfounded.

"Home certainly isn't this rowboat, Ginny. We're only about a hundred and fifty feet from that island straight ahead. That's where we're headed," said Brad.

"Ginny," Chelsea questioned, "do you have the horseshoe?"

I flexed the fingers of my left hand and brought it forward. "I didn't drop it this time. But we're still not home," I answered as I opened my hand to reassure my cousins I had the horseshoe.

Brad warned sternly, "Don't hold it near the water. That's all we need, to lose the horseshoe in this river."

"He's right," agreed Chelsea. "Put it in your pocket, or better yet, let's try to travel again!"

"I'm for that," I said, looking at Brad to see what he wanted to do.

"Not so fast. Let's check out this island first. These trees look normal, no heavy foliage or vines. We might be in the present, just not at home," Brad suggested.

For the first time I took a good look at the island. He was right. I recognized maples, oaks and elms. I could even make out wildflowers growing near the water's edge. It looked peaceful.

"A deer, look!" Chelsea shouted. "There's another one and another. Maybe we should just explore the island before we travel again."

"Under one condition," I demanded, "no Indians, prehistoric or any other kind."

"It's a deal," Brad consented as he rowed faster toward the island.

As we drew closer, I could see and smell honeysuckle and wild roses. Blackberry and raspberry bushes, sagging with the weight of fruit, laced the island's edge. Fish darted from the reeds to the boat, easily visible in the clear water. The gobbling of wild turkeys, the chirping of birds, and the chattering of squirrels filled the air.

"The current is pulling us around the bend. I'll try and dock there," Brad said as he pulled in the oars and just let the boat drift.

"Oh! Oh, my!" gasped Chelsea from the front of the boat. "This is beautiful. We've found paradise."

"I can't see . . . ." I began as the boat gently swung around the bend and a landing came into view.

Chelsea was right. It was a beautiful sight. Six pink and white marble steps rose majestically out of the water to a wide platform on the shore. Two massive columns, at least twenty feet tall, stood on either end of

The South Charleston or Criel Mound was excavated in 1883 by the Smithsonian Institute. Thirteen skeletons were discovered, most of them in a large log tomb at the base of the mound, along with a few grave offerings. This mound, the second largest in the state of West Virginia, was built about A.D. 1 by the Adena-Hopwell culture.

the platform. A wide dirt road, a sweeping fan-shaped lawn, several gravel paths, and acres of flowers lay beyond the columns.

Thump, thump, thump, the rowboat hit against the lowest step. Brad sat up, dazed.

"Come on," Chelsea said, rocking the boat as she jumped up. "I think I'm going to like this place. Let's go!"

"Where can we be?" said a puzzled Brad to himself.

"The horseshoe is safe and sound in my pocket. Let's go and find out," I encouraged him. "And if we don't like it, we can always leave."

The boat almost tipped over as Chelsea leaped onto the steps. I waited until the boat steadied before I stepped out. Brad placed the oars in the bottom of the boat, picked up the line and climbed onto the steps. He moored the boat securely to an iron ring.

"It's even more beautiful from up here," Chelsea cried from the platform. "I think there is a house in the distance, a big white one."

I dashed up the steps next to my cousin. "Yes, I see it. This must be an old plantation. Brad, this is really neat."

Brad, still with a dazed look on his face, climbed the steps slowly. He paused to look in all directions from each step. He stepped onto the platform. "I don't know what to make of this. I can put the golden horseshoe with West Virginia, but I can't put this place anywhere in West Virginia," he said.

"I see someone," Chelsea said, shading her eyes.

"Where?" Brad and I asked simultaneously as we turned in the direction Chelsea faced.

"In the road, near the right edge. It looks like a boy. He steps into the woods at times. See!" Chelsea continued in an excited voice. "There he is again. He's coming this way."

Chelsea began to wave frantically trying to attract the stranger's attention. The figure in the distance paused and then returned the greeting. He moved into the middle of the road and quickened his steps.

He appeared to be about Chelsea's age, average build, and dark haired. His clothes were out of sight. He wore tight dark pants that buttoned just below the knees and a white gauze shirt with a wide collar. There were no buttons on the loose-fitting shirt and the sleeves were rolled to the elbows. His bare feet displayed a film of dust up to the calves of his legs. His hair, as long as Chelsea's, was tied neatly at the nape of his neck with a black grogram ribbon.

He stopped five feet away from us and stared. "A pleasant day to you, sir, and to the ladies. We weren't expecting guests until tomorrow eve.'' After several awkward seconds of silence, he continued in a dignified voice, ''I'm most sorry the boatmen were not here to help you disembark. If you will please tarry, I will have Ramon bring a carriage.''

''N–n–no,'' Brad sputtered, ''That won't be necessary.''

''Yes, it will,'' Chelsea piped up. ''I would love to ride a carriage and . . .''

Brad tried to quiet Chelsea with a frown as he interrupted, ''Eh, we came early. A carriage won't be necessary. Just let Ramon go on with what he was doing.''

''As you say, sir. Do you wish to journey to the main house?'' the boy asked. ''It is too early for tea, but Lizzy will provide you with refreshments.''

''That sounds great,'' Brad responded with more control, ''but could you show us around first? We'd like to see more of the island.''

''Forgive me, please.'' He bowed slightly. ''I should have known this was your primary trip. I don't remember meeting you earlier, but my parents do entertain many guests. If you wish to see the island, I must go for Ramon. My mama would never permit guests to walk such a distance.''

''You live here?'' I asked.

''Yes, I have always lived here. I am Dominick. I was born a few months before my parents moved onto the island. My younger brother Harman, Jr. was born in the mansion.''

Chelsea asked boldly, ''Dominick what?''

''She's not good at pronouncing names,'' Brad interjected. ''She wants to make sure she says it just right.''

''Dominick Blennerhassett,'' the boy replied. ''Blen-ner-has-sett.''

''Dominick Blennerhassett,'' Chelsea repeated. ''Are you French? That sounds French, doesn't it, Ginny?''

''No, my ancestors are English,'' said Dominick. ''My parents came . . .''

''Harmon Blennerhassett and Aaron Burr!'' whispered Brad with a gasp. ''This is Blennerhassett Island.''

''I beg your humble pardon, sir,'' Dominick said. ''Did I understand you to say your name is Burr?''

''No, no, I am acquainted with Mr. Burr,'' Brad responded as he greeted Dominick with a firm handshake. ''My name is Brad Brown, and this is my sister, Chelsea, and my cousin, Ginny Lucas.''

Dominick clicked his bare heels together and bowed in front of Chelsea. "Chelsea, what a lovely name for a lovely maiden," he said.

He then turned toward me, clicked his bare heels again, bowed and said, "Ginny Lucas, I am most honored to greet you and your cousins. Welcome to my island home."

He turned toward Brad and continued in an adult tone, "I thought surely you must be acquainted with Mr. Burr—the unusual, eh, I mean unique style of your clothing and the foreign speech pattern. You must tell me about your country. My parents say we will journey to your country next spring, once the fighting is over."

"You bet. We sure will," promised Chelsea, smiling at the handsome boy.

Dominick asked, "Will Mr. Burr be arriving early also? I must inform my parents . . ."

"He's coming as scheduled," Brad answered. "We just decided to come early."

"Good. Papa would be disappointed if he did not arrive. Shall we be off to the kitchen for refreshments? I can send Ramon later for your bags," offered Dominick.

"We didn't bring bags on this trip," I explained to a shocked looking Dominick. "Eh, Mr. Burr will bring them with him."

"How thoughtful of him. Ladies, if you care to take my arm we will venture to the kitchen before we tour the island," said Dominick. He stood between Chelsea and me with bent elbows extended.

We linked arms and started toward a gravel path with Brad following behind us. The path Dominick chose, one of three leading toward the main house, was bordered by hawthorn hedge. To the right of the hedge were acres of flowers arranged in colorful patterns.

"That's beautiful," I remarked. "Do your mom and dad take care of all this?"

"My parents do not tend gardens," Dominick answered in a haughty tone. "My papa brought Mr. Taylor from Lancashire, England, to oversee the gardens. The servants follow his directions."

"Oh," I said softly.

"We don't have big flower gardens or servants in our country," Chelsea explained.

"No servants, are you sure?" Dominick questioned.

"No, she's not," Brad replied and shot a scornful look toward

Chelsea. "I believe, servants are allowed and welcomed. Of course, your papa and Mr. Burr will make those laws."

The wide lawn and colorful flower gardens provided an appropriate setting for the mansion ahead. The main house, two stories high, dominated the crescent-shaped manor. Forty foot porticoes (columned porches) connected a single floor dwelling on the right and a larger structure on the left to the main house.

Dominick led us toward the large structure on the left. "We'll pause here, if you do not mind, to take refreshments in the kitchen, before I show you around the island," he said.

"Who lives over there?" Chelsea asked, pointing to the single floor building about the size of a garage.

"No one lives there," Dominick laughed. "That is Papa's laboratory and library. Papa likes to practice alchemy [chemistry]. Sometimes there are explosions, so Mama insisted the laboratory be away from the main house. But he is pretty good. He concocts potions that help with sicknesses."

I asked, "Is your father a doctor?"

"No," Dominick answered, "he is a lawyer and a businessman. He is also a musician and composer. You will hear him play the pieces he has written for the cello at the party tomorrow eve. He jolly likes to amuse his guests."

We stepped onto the portico on the left and turned toward an open door. Dominick led us into an enormous kitchen that covered the ground floor. A huge fireplace, with an opening taller than Brad, dominated the center of the room. Two black caldrons (kettles), hanging from iron bars, bubbled over a low fire. A two foot piece of curved copper, serving as a reflector oven, stood in front of the fireplace guarding a half roasted leg of lamb. An assortment of iron pots and skillets, spits, giant forks and ladles dotted the shelves above the hearth. Two stacked wall ovens stood at the right, flanked by long handled wooden bread paddles. Various vegetables, fruits, and herbs were hung from the ceiling to dry. Candle and soap frames were neatly stacked against the right wall. A spinning wheel and a basket of wool, ready to be spun, caught the light from a back window. Rows of crockery, labeled as assorted jams, jellies, honey, syrup, and spices, filled the shelves on the left. Two butter churns were set near a large cupboard with decorated tin doors. One smaller locked cabinet butted against the large cupboard. A long wooden work table, scrubbed pale grey like the spotless floor, held racks of knives, serving platters, and dishes under its worn top. The aroma of roasting meat, the rich smell of baked bread, the sweet smell of syrup and the spicy scent of herbs filled the pleasant room.

"Lizzy, Lizzy," Dominick called in a friendly voice, "I have some guests in need of refreshments, please."

The scrape of a chair and the sound of footsteps came from the loft overhead. "Now, Masta Dom, yo know yor mama don't allow me to surv guests in ma kitchen," remarked a small black woman climbing down backward from the loft.

As she turned and looked at us, her eyes widened and her mouth dropped open. "Where you from?" she demanded, looking sharply at Brad. She moved protectively between us and Dominick.

"Lizzy," Dominick scolded, "they're friends of Mr. Burr. They just arrived early." He lowered his voice and whispered just to her, "Besides, no one my age has come with Mr. Burr before. Be cordial to them, Lizzy. I relish their visit."

"Yo mama don't say nuttin' 'bout early guests, Masta Dom. An' she gone to Marietta. What did yo papa say?" Lizzy questioned Dominick as she continued to glare at us.

"Papa went quail hunting this morning," said Dominick in a haughty tone, "so that leaves me in charge. I will offer hospitality to our guests." He softened his tone, smiled warmly at Lizzy and asked tenderly, "Lizzy, can't we have some refreshments here in the kitchen, please?"

She returned his smile with a broad grin and reached for chairs to put around the work table. "Masta Dom," she said, "you better not be up to no good. And when yo mama and papa gits back, yo better take these'uns to the big house right away."

Looking at us, she said, "I's got hot tea and fresh milk, hoe cakes and spoon bread. You'uns can have 'em with syrup, molasses, honey or jam."

Chelsea mumbled to me, "No pizza or bologna and mustard? I'd give anything for a hot dog and a Snickers bar."

"Dominick," I asked, "what is your favorite snack, eh, I mean your favorite refreshment?"

"I enjoy a hoe cake with honey and sweet milk," Dominick responded.

"Sounds good to me," Brad said.

Chelsea just moaned.

"We'll try that," I agreed. "Dominick, will you join us?"

"I would be most happy," he said, as he led us to chairs around the table.

Lizzy set pewter plates, mugs, and flatware in front of us. She carried a platter of what looked like fried cornbread biscuits and a pitcher of milk to Dominick. As Dominick passed the hoecakes and milk around, Lizzy returned with a crock of honey. Dominick used a wooden stick to ladle the honey onto his hoecakes. He spread the honey like syrup, cut the two cakes, into bite-size pieces, and began to eat. We followed his example.

Chelsea exclaimed, "Hey, Dominick, these are really good!"

"The best I've had in a long time," Brad offered.

"Do have more," Dominick suggested as he passed the platter a second time. "I am pleased you relish our hospitality."

After the snack, we thanked Lizzy for the food and began to clear the table. Dominick just watched as I stacked the plates and Brad returned the honey crock to its shelf.

"No, suh, no," Lizzy objected. "I's do de work in dis kitchen. Now you'uns go on with Masta Dom to see de island."

Dominick insisted as he stood in the doorway, "This way, please. I will show you the main house before we tour the island."

We followed the portico and entered the parlor on the left side of the mansion. The room looked light and airy with its high ceiling and lace curtains. A gold-trimmed molding around the ceiling, a thick Oriental carpet on the floor and a fireplace of dark marble added to the richness of the room. A harpsicord, viola, and cello were placed near the window to enable the musicians to have adequate lighting. Paintings in ornate frames were hung on all walls.

"This parlor is for entertaining. Papa and Mama both enjoy music, and they play also. Papa insists I learn the harpsichord and cello, but I do not like to practice," Dominick said.

"I'm with you," nodded Chelsea. "What's behind the huge doors?"

"The dining room," Dominick answered. He pulled open two enormous walnut doors with silver handles. "Come, I will show you."

The dining room had dark walls with a white plaster molding trimmed in gold. The large mahogany table, complete with highback chairs, was set for forty people. The two long, mirrored sideboards held cut glass, fine china, and sparkling silver. A shimmering crystal chandelier, able to hold one hundred candles, hung majestically from the ceiling. It reminded me of a palace or a movie star's home.

"As you note, Mama is already preparing for the gala tomorrow eve." Dominick motioned toward the table. "I hope Mr. Burr remembers your parcels when he arrives. We all must wear our finest for the special occasion."

Chelsea began, "What spec . . . "

"I'm sure he will," Brad said.

Dominick led us through another pair of walnut doors into a foyer. Twin staircases, leading to the second floor, curved above a mirrored chandelier. The dark cherry banister cast a pattern of shadows on the pale blue carpet throughout the hall. From an open door on the right, I saw a room paneled in rich walnut with several paintings and a mirror framed in gold.

Dominick remarked casually, "That's the drawing room where my parents receive guests."

"Where do you hang out?" I asked.

"Hang out? Hang? I am most sorry. I do not understand," replied Dominick.

"Where do you stay, you know, live? Where do you spend time when it's just you and your family?" Brad explained.

"Oh, I am clear now." Dominick smiled. "There is a room behind the parlor where we take our meals, and our sitting room is behind the drawing room."

Dominick led us to the back of the hall and into these smaller rooms. They were cozier and more comfortable, but still richly decorated.

Taking quick steps toward the window of the sitting room, Dominick pulled back a lace curtain. "It is Mama. I will show you the bed chambers later. First, I must present you to Mama."

We followed Dominick through the sitting room, hallway, dining room, and parlor. We stepped onto the portico to watch a woman dressed in a flowing red dress and red hat with a long white plume galloping sidesaddle toward us. She was riding so fast I thought she was going to ride into us. Instead, within three feet of Dominick the horse reared twice and stopped.

The tall, lovely, brown-haired woman swooped down from the horse laughing. She gave Dominick a warm hug and said, "Look, I won again!"

We realized what she meant when another rider, a modestly dressed black man, came rushing toward the portico. He pulled his horse to a stop at least fifteen feet away and let it approach Mrs. Blennerhassett's mount.

46

"Reed, that was a great race," said Mrs. Blennerhasset warmly. "Curry and feed both horses before you put them away."

"Yes 'um," Reed answered with his head down. Without looking at her he said, "I's to protect yo. If you 'ens run off like dat and git hert, Masta Blennerhassett be mighty mad. He woop me good, Miss Maggie."

"Don't you worry about that, Reed. I'll never get hurt on a horse," consoled Mrs. Blennerhassett. "You just take care of the horses like I said, and I'll deal with my husband."

Turning toward us, she studied us carefully. She raised her left eyebrow and tilted her head. "And who are our guests, Dominick?"

"They are from Mr. Burr's country, Mama." Dominick's voice picked up an air of authority as he introduced us. "This is Master Brad Brown, traveling with his beautiful sister, Chelsea, and his lovely cousin, Ginny Lucas." With each name, he gestured toward that person and bowed.

The expression on Mrs. Blennerhassett's face did not change as she curtsied before each of us. Her eyes looked into our souls, as she questioned Brad. "You know Mr. Burr?" she asked.

"Eh," Brad swallowed hard, "yes, madam, I . . . we do."

"Mr. Burr has never sent a party before his visits," she continued. "Is there a reason you were dispatched?"

"Yes, madam." Brad suddenly sounded confident. "I apprenticed under my father building gunboats. Mr. Burr has entrusted me to examine the work being done here. Eh, he allowed me to bring my sister and cousin on the journey; this is their first trip back East."

Mrs. Blennerhassett's face softened and she smiled. "That explains why you are here. Dominick, these guests need to be quartered near the boatyard. She looked at Chelsea and me, then suggested, "No, wait. Take Mr. Brown to the boatyard and have Lizzy make room in the servants' hall for the young ladies."

"But, Mama, the servants' hall? Are you sure?" questioned Dominick.

Mrs. Blennershasset answered him sharply, "Yes, I am very sure."

"Yes, Mama," an embarrassed Dominick mumbled.

"Mr. Brown," Mrs. Blennerhassert's tone became serious, "my husband and I will expect a complete report from you after your examination."

Brad responded, "Yes, ma'am, as soon as possible."

"Please all of you, join us for the evening meal at seven," requested Mrs. Blennerhassett looking then at Chelsea and me.

Together Chelsea and I curtsied as if that was the customary thing for us to do. Brad sighed as Mrs. Blennerhassett turned to enter the mansion.

Dominick, looking embarrassed, said, "I am sorry. I thought you would be staying in the big house. Excuse me, please. I will speak to my mother, then I will return."

Before Dominick could enter the door, Chelsea and I simultaneously began questioning Brad, "Who is this Aaron Burr? What is this boat business? Are we in danger? Is Dominick . . ."

"Wait, one at a time," said Brad. "This is what I know about Aaron Burr. He was vice president under Thomas Jefferson. In fact, Jefferson must still be president; I guess it's about 1805 or 1806. Burr is going to try and create a new country from part of Texas and Mexico. He needs money, weapons, troops, and boats to send this new army down the Ohio River, to the Mississippi River, and then on to New Orleans."

Chelsea interrupted, "What does that have to do with Dominick or his parents?"

"Dominick's father," Brad continued in a patient voice, "Harman Blennerhassett, has a lot of money. You heard Dominick say his dad was a businessman; well, he plans to support the army so Burr can set up a new country. In return, Burr promised the Blennerhassetts they would rule the new land, like a king and queen."

"Neat," I said. "So why do you look so down, Brad?"

Brad answered firmly, "It's not neat; it's treason! That territory belongs to the United States. Burr also plans to start a war between his new country and the United States. Luckily, it doesn't work. In fact, Jefferson will send an army to capture Burr and Blennerhasset here on the island before the plan goes into action." He paused and lowered his voice. "This mansion will be looted, destroyed and burned. The army will leave the island in ruins."

"What about Dominick?" I asked, choking. "What about his family?"

"He'll be all right, eh, he's not killed if that's what you mean. His dad will go to jail but will be released in about a year. Dominick, his little brother, and his mother will see the mansion destroyed before they are able to escape. The family will reunite and build another plantation in Mississippi."

48

"Treason, traitors," Chelsea mumbled. "Do you think Dominick knows that his father is a traitor? That he will go to jail?"

Brad answered, "No, neither Dominick nor his father has any idea at this time what will happen. Mr. Blennerhassett is just interested in the money he'll make. Not too many of his business deals have been successful, but Mr. Burr convinced him this would work and he would make a fortune."

"Maybe, just maybe," Chelsea began in an excited voice, "we could explain what Mr. Burr is up to, and Mr. Blennerhassett will back out of the deal. Then this mansion wouldn't be destroyed. Dominick wouldn't be humiliated and, you know, have to move and all that?"

"Do you think it would work?" I asked, looking at Brad.

"Get real, you two," Brad replied in a irritated tone. "Now who in the world would believe us? 'We've come through time, folks, and boy do we have news for you! Nobody, but nobody would take us seriously. Besides, we can't change history."

I felt really dumb after Brad's snide remark, so I just agreed, "I think you are right, Brad."

Chelsea wasn't about to let her brother get by with his scolding remarks. "What makes you an authority on what people will believe? And, Mr. Bigshot, how do you know we can't change history? I bet if I explained this situation to Dominick, he told his dad, and Ginny showed him the horseshoe that . . . "

"Shhh, Chelsea," I interrupted, "here comes Dominick."

"Just keep quiet, Sis," Brad warned under his breath.

Dominick didn't seem as cheerful now as he was earlier. He marched past Chelsea and me as if we were invisible. With a serious look on his face, he remarked to Brad, "Mama said I should take you immediately to the boatyard. Your sister and cousin will be lodged at the blockhouse. They should be more comfortable there than in the servants' hall."

"Dominick . . . " Chelsea interrupted but was ignored.

Dominick continued, "I will retain a wagon and driver from the stables and escort you to the designated areas. I trust your visit here will be honorable." With a nod to Brad, Dominick turned briskly down a path and was out of sight within minutes.

"Well, I never!" Chelsea fumed, placing both hands on her hips. "And to think I was worried about him. What a jerk!"

"You don't know what his mother said to him. Maybe it's not his fault," I explained. "Besides, you do have to admit we look weird. I haven't seen anyone else on this plantation with jeans and T-shirts."

"I know that! Are you going to be like Brad and talk to me like I'm stupid?" Chelsea snapped angrily.

"No, it's just . . . " I tried to explain, but Chelsea turned her back and folded her arms across her chest.

"We can't blame Dominick," said Brad. "He's been very decent to us. His mother is just smart enough to realize that we are really strange and not people from Mr. Burr's country. I think she is aware of what could happen to her family if the American government found out about what is going on here."

"You were the one who had to open his big mouth about checking the dumb gunboats." said Chelsea as she turned toward Brad. "If you had kept your mouth shut, we would probably be staying in the mansion, and going to the big party tomorrow night. But oh, no, my brother the brain . . . "

"Oh, Chelsea," I said, "there's no use blaming Brad. Who knows, we may still get to go to the party tomorrow night. Anyway, we get to come back for dinner tonight."

"I don't know if I want to come for dinner," Chelsea pouted, "especially after the way 'la Dominijerk' is acting."

Brad teased, "Smart boy, that Dominick. He only speaks to people with brains."

I had to chuckle at Brad's remark.

The sound of creaking wagon wheels caught our attention. Coming toward us was a flatbed farm wagon driven by an elderly, white-haired black man. Dominick sat next to the man and balanced himself by holding on to the brake handle. the two farmhorses looked worn and dirty like the wagon they pulled. The servant, clad only in kneepants, pulled the wagon to a halt, and Dominick pulled the brake.

Dominick jumped down from the wagon and addressed Brad. "You ride up front. I will ride with the ladies in the back. We will transport you to the boatyard first."

Brad stepped on the hub of the wagon wheel and climbed up into the seat. "Shotgun, that's me," he said.

Somhow I became invisible as Dominick gazed into Chelsea's eyes. He took her hand and began apologizing, "I am so sorry about your accommodations. I trust you will not be too uncomfortable. My mama is suspicious of Mr. Burr . . . eh, some people. Within a short period of time, after Mama gets to know you better, you must return to the big house. Please forgive . . . this . . . this uncivilized move.''

"Oh, Dominick," Chelsea said, clasping her other hand over his, "don't you worry at all. I really don't mind. Besides, I will still get to see you, won't I? There are so many things we need to talk about.''

Dominick replied, "Certainly. You may grow weary of seeing me.''

"And I will get to see you too, won't I?" I said, just to let them know I was alive and standing within ten inches of their private world.

Dominick's face reddened and Chelsea dropped his hand. "Oh, yes, Ginny," Dominick stammered. "We . . . we, the three of us, will find amusement, while Brad does his reports at the boatyard. Allow me to assist you onto the wagon. Mama has sent Vivian to prepare the blockhouse.''

Dominick cupped his hands for Chelsea and me to use as a step. We scooted toward the middle of the wagon and leaned back against two bales of hay. Dominick jumped onto the back of the wagon and signaled the driver to leave.

"Shall we ride the back?" Dominick asked, extending one hand to Chelsea and brushing straw off the wagon floor with the other.

Chelsea poked me with her elbow and mumbled, "Here's my chance." She barely had time to seat herself close to Dominick before the wagon jolted to a start.

I was invisible again as the wagon started over the knoll. We passed the long white stable and a two story barn. These buildings and a two acre vegetable garden could not be seen from the mansion. We pulled onto a smooth dirt road, probably a continuation of the road at the landing, and started around the island. We rode by apple and peach orchards, bee hives, tobacco fields, walnut groves and corn fields. As many as forty blacks, men, women and children, were working in the tobacco and corn fields, while two white men stood near by with guns. It was then I realized these people weren't servants, they were slaves. The sound of gunshots startled me.

Dominick stopped talking to Chelsea and commanded, "Zeke, stop here.''

The wagon came to a halt, and Dominick jumped off the side. Three rapid gunshots were heard close by.

Dominick ordered, "Zeke, Papa, and Jeb must be hunting quail near the river. Go tell Papa three of Mr. Burr's guests have arrived early. We'll wait here.''

51

"Yes 'um, Masta Dom," said Zeke, as he reached over and pulled the brake. "I's say t'ree of Masta Burr's guests cum erly and you 'ens waitin here on de road."

Zeke climbed carefully down from the wagon and began to shuffle into the woods in the direction of the gunshots. Dominick motioned for Brad, Chelsea, and me to leave the wagon.

When the old slave was out of sight Dominick turned and faced Brad. "Zeke will be gone a long time. You must leave now," he warned.

"Why?" Brad questioned.

"Mama thinks you are a spy. The guards at the boatyard will hold you until Mr. Burr arrives. If you are a spy, and Chelsea has been telling me most unusual tales, you will be shot," said Dominick.

"I'm not a spy," gasped Brad. "Chelsea, I told you to keep your mouth shut."

"You do not threaten her," demanded Dominick stepping between Brad and Chelsea.

"Brad, I've been trying to explain to Dominick about the horseshoe and traveling in time. Ginny, Ginny, show him the horseshoe," Chelsea said desperately.

I waited until Brad nodded, before I pulled the horseshoe out of my pocket. I explained, "One of the diamonds is missing. On our last trip I lost the horseshoe in a cave. When we found it, a diamond was gone. Dominick, I don't know what Chelsea has been telling you, but Brad isn't a spy."

Dominick studied the horseshoe with a confused look on his face. He looked at Chelsea and then said to Brad, "I have not studied abroad. From my books here I have never heard of time travel, but my papa is a learned man. I must discuss this with him. I trust what you say to be true."

He turned toward Chelsea and asked, "My sweet, do you think me ignorant of science or a fool to believe fantasy?"

Chelsea answered, "Neither. Trust me, Dominick. You must convince your father of Mr. Burr's conspiracy. I'm sure he is an honest man and will want nothing to do with Mr. Burr. If Ginny. . . . "

"Horses," interrupted Dominick, "guards from the boatyard. Hurry, into the woods."

We followed Dominick through a prickly blackberry thicket to a clump of beech trees. We ducked behind a huge tree with honeysuckle

52

vines cascading from its branches. The four guards stopped at the wagon. Reed, the slave that came in with Mrs. Blennerhassett, was with them.

"Dat's de wagon," Reed said. "Do you think dey's done away with Masta Dom? Miss Maggie be turribul sad if'n enything happen to Masta Dom."

A thin white man with a pox-marked face and straggly beard barked, "Spread out, men. They're on foot, so they can't get too far. Order them to halt; if they don't—shoot. Watch out for the Blennerhassett boy; we can't afford to harm him."

"It's time to leave, Ginny," Brad whispered.

I nodded and handed him the horseshoe. Dominick just stared at Chelsea.

"Come with us, please?" Chelsea asked Dominick.

"I . . . I would not fit in your world," said Dominick. "Besides, you are still here. Why don't you stay with me?"

Chelsea looked at Brad to help her decide. With tears in her eyes she whispered, "I can't . . . I wouldn't fit in your world, either."

Dominick wiped the tears from the corners of her eyes and kissed her gently on the cheek. He untied the black ribbon from his hair and reached for Chelsea's hand. He kissed her open palm, put the ribbon in her hand, and closed her fingers over the ribbon.

"Chelsea," urged Brad, "you've got to move with us over to the clearing. We've got to get the horseshoe in the light. Come on, now."

Dominick turned to Brad. "I will rush onto the road and lead the guards toward the river."

Without looking back at any of us, he darted through the thicket toward the dusty road. Within seconds I heard him yell at the guards to follow him.

We reached the clearing, and Brad held the horseshoe toward the light. He turned it from side to side, letting the sun blaze on the gems. Nothing happened.

"Here, Ginny, you try," Brad said as he handed me the horseshoe. "You've been holding it the last two times when we traveled."

I took the horseshoe and held it directly between me and the sun. I turned it to pick up the light. Nothing happened. I was beginning to worry. "Here, Chelsea, you try," I said.

I put the horseshoe in Chelsea's hand. She looked at it and began to cry. She wiped the tears from the horseshoe and gasped, "Oh, no! We've lost another diamond! That's why it won't work."

I grabbed the horseshoe and held it to the light. "She's right, Brad; another stone is missing. Do you think that's why we're still here?"

Brad's voice was cracking. "It's got to work. Hold it higher, Ginny. Move over this way. Hurry!"

I held the horseshoe over my head into the sunlight. I turned it back and forth, again and again. My arm was begining to ache and the sun was blinding in my eyes. I kept turning the golden horseshoe. All of a sudden I started spinning. The lights began to flash. There it was, high above my head, the blazing horseshoe.

Facts

1. Aaron Burr, former vice president under Thomas Jefferson, and Harman Blennerhassett plotted to create a separate country in the western United States. Blennerhassett provided the money for this venture in exchange for the opportunity to rule the new country.
2. Thomas Jefferson sent troops to Blennerhassett Island to capture Aaron Burr and Herman Blennerhassett before a new country could be formed. Both men were charged with treason, but were later released.
3. The army sent by Thomas Jefferson ruined the mansion and grounds. Later a flood completely destroyed the house.
4. The restoration and completion of the mansion on Blennerhassett Island cost $768,000.00.
5. Tours from Parkersburg, West Virginia, by ferry, to the island are now available.
6. Harman Blennerhassett composed music, played the viola and cello, and experimented in chemistry. His laboratory was located off the right portico from the main house.
7. The exterior and interior descriptions of the mansion are accurate.
8. Harman and Margaret Blennerhassett had five children. Dominick and Harman, Jr., were born on the island. A third son, Joseph Lewis, was born at the plantation, LaCahe, on the Mississippi River. There were two daughters; both died in infancy.
9. Dominick was ten or eleven years old during the Burr-Blennerhassett conspiracy.

10. Margaret Blennerhassett, an accomplished horsewoman, is remembered today as a poetess. Her poem "The Deserted Isle" described the beauty and destruction of the mansion on Blennerhassett Island.

Blennerhassett Island, located in the Ohio River near Parkersburg, West Virginia.

The restored Blennerhassett Mansion hosts the only live historical drama to be performed at an original site. The audience is ferried to and from the island for each performance.

55

Interior of the restored kitchen of the Blennerhassett Mansion, located in the left wing.

Chapter 5

Harpers Ferry

I wasn't frightened by the spinning or the flashing lights. I knew we were traveling; I only hoped this time we would end up at home. The horseshoe came nearer and nearer, I grabbed it with a fierce determination to stop it. I held tightly as the revolving feeling came to a halt. The lights ceased to flash, so I blinked open my eyes.

It wasn't Grandma's house. It was a two-story, red brick house that set on a knoll above a cemetery. I was leaning against worn stone steps that led to a wooden porch with a glass pane doorway. Ornate black iron railings trimmed the veranda that stretched across the front and sides of the house. Two empty rockers, a wicker settee, one wooden end table, and two deacon's benches were casually placed on the porch. The front lawn was shaded by two huge maple trees and divided by a stone path from the cemetery to the porch.

I got up slowly and called softly, "Brad, Chelsea, where are you?"

There was no answer. I moved a few feet away from the front porch and called again. "Brad, Chelsea, can you hear me?"

I held my breath as I started around the side of the house. There they were! Brad was sitting upright rubbing his eyes. Chelsea was sprawled on the ground next to two white wooden doors. I ran toward her and tried to help her up.

"Chelsea, Chelsea," I whispered, "wake up. Come on. Answer me." I patted her hands and shook her head.

"The neck," Chelsea moaned. "Don't you dare break my neck, Ginny Lucas."

"Thank God you're okay," I sighed.

"Okay except for whiplash. I hope you have a good lawyer," Chelsea teased. "Hey! Anybody know where we are this time?" she continued as she looked up at the towering brick house.

Brad answered, "Next to a cemetery. Maybe we should check the tombstones and make sure we're not already in it."

"Brad," I scolded, "I don't think that's so funny."

"We're not home, and I don't think that's so funny," Brad snapped back.

"Tell him off, Ginny," prodded Chelsea. "See what a smart aleck he can be."

"That's not going to do us any good," I reminded her. "I'm ready to go home. I'm tired of this traveling bit. Here, you take it," I said as I handed the horseshoe to Brad.

"I don't think it matters who has the horseshoe," Brad responded in a more pleasant tone. "You keep it, Ginny. We're going to be all right. We'll make it back to Grandma's."

"We may as well take a look around while we're here," Chelsea said, rising to her feet. "Doors in the ground? Who lives underground?" Chelsea stared at the double white doors.

Brad lifted one of the unlocked doors and stepped into the threshold. He turned and said, "It's a root cellar. This place is loaded with apples, potatoes, pickles in barrels, and some strange looking things, that I guess you could eat. Anyone care for an apple?"

Chelsea warned sternly, "Brad Brown, you'd better get out of there. What if someone catches you?"

"For what?" Brad asked, stepping out of the cellar and shutting the door softly.

"For breaking and entering, Dumbo," snapped Chelsea.

"Have an apple on me," laughed Brad as he tossed an apple to Chelsea and then one to me.

"Let's see if there is anyone home," I suggested. "Maybe we could explain what has been happening to us . . . and maybe somebody will know what we should do."

"Fat chance," Brad said.

"You know, big brother," Chelsea began, "you're beginning to sound like the voice of doom."

Brad said, "I really don't mean to sound so negative, but face facts. First, who would believe us? Second, if they did believe us,what could anyone do to help?"

Chelsea turned toward me and sneered. "Translated, that means

58

'If I, Brad the Great, can't figure out how to get home, then no one else in the world could possibly figure out a way to get us home.' Right?''

Brad rolled his eyes, folded his arms across his chest. "It's wonderful having you for a sister," he said.

"You two, knock it off," I said. "I'm going to knock on the door and try to find someone to help us. You can stay here and argue if you want." I turned and marched toward the front of the house without looking back.

Brad called, "Wait up! We're coming!"

Together we ascended the three worn limestone steps onto the wooden porch. The porch boards creaked under our weight. An empty cane rocker squeaked and swayed in a soft breeze as we crossed the veranda. I knocked on the door and waited. There was no answer. I rapped louder, making the glass panes rattle. Still no answer. I cupped my hands around my eyes and pressed against the glass, trying to see through the thin gauze curtain that covered the door.

"Hello! Hello!" I shouted. I turned the brass knob, and the door opened easily. "Anybody home?" I called. Dead silence.

Chelsea looked over my shoulder. "This is spooky."

I moved into the hallway. A simple uncarpeted stairway led to the second floor, and opened double doors on the right revealed a sitting room. A burgundy Victorian loveseat, adorned with a crocheted doily across its back, was visible from the foyer. I walked slowly into the parlor.

"Hello," I called, "anybody home?"

"It's deserted," commented Brad as he walked over to an upright piano sitting in the corner. He seated himself on the swivel stool and started playing chopsticks.

"Do make yourself right at home," offered Chelsea. "Don't worry about all the trouble we could get into by being in this house."

I gazed around the room trying to figure out the time period and location from the furnishings. A pot belly stove and black ash can stood in front of a sealed fireplace. A brass chandelier that had been converted from candle power to gas hung from the ceiling. Two overstuffed armchairs, separated by a circular table holding a gas lamp, set across from the loveseat. Crocheted doilies protected the arms and head rests of the chairs while a braided rug covered the hardwood floor. A library table holding seven volumns was placed behind the loveseat and a butler's table with a Bible and folded newspaper . . .

59

"Look at this!" I shouted, picking up the newspaper. I read aloud, *"Harpers Chronicle,* October 16, 1859; the headlines say 'Arsenal and Hostages Held Captive.' "

Brad and Chelsea stood behind me as I read aloud from the newspaper. " 'John Brown, abolitionist from Kansas, with eighteen men, captured the federal arsenal and rifle works at Harpers Ferry, Virginia. Telegraph wires were cut, a passenger train seized, and four hostages held captive. Col. Lewis W. Washington, the great-grandnephew of George Washington, is reported to be one of the hostages. According to eyewitnesses, John Brown, carrying a Bible in his right hand and waving the famous Washington sword (stolen from the colonel's home) in his left, has turned the arsenal into a fort for his band of raiders. United States Marines, under the command of Col. Robert E. Lee and Lt. J. E. B. Stuart, have been dispatched to the Virginia railroad community.' "

Brad whistled low. "That tells us a lot. It's 1859 and we're somewhere near or in Harpers Ferry, Virginia."

"It also tells us the horseshoe goofed. We should be in West Virginia, not Virginia," Chelsea said.

Brad snapped, "We were Virginia at one time, Chelsea. Didn't you learn anything in school? We don't become West Virginia until 18 . . eh, 1860 . . . 1863. Yeah, 1863."

"I know that. I just forgot," replied Chelsea.

"Wait a minute," I demanded. "Neither Robert E. Lee nor J. E. B. Stuart was in the United States Marines. They fought with the South, the Confederacy. This newspaper couldn't be right."

"Ginny," Brad began, "the Civil War hasn't happened yet. The country is still arguing over slavery. That's why John Brown went to Harpers Ferry, to capture the arsenal and rifle works. Ammunition, weapons, and other war-time supplies are stored in arsenals. Guns are made in factories. John Brown planned on taking all these supplies, freeing the slaves in Virginia, giving them weapons, and leading a huge revolt."

"You still haven't explained to me about Lee and Stuart? I know for a fact they were Southern officers," I insisted.

"You're right. They were during the Civil War," agreed Brad. "But when Lee graduated from West Point, he joined the United States Marines. J. E. B. Stuart was also a career man in the marines. They really did lead the regiment that captured John Brown. Later on, when Virginia se . . . "

"I remember now," interrupted Chelsea. "When Virginia secedes from the Union, Lee and Stuart fight with the South."

"At least you remember something from history class," replied Brad.

The distant sound of gunshots pierced the walls of the old house. I looked at my cousins. We ran to the front windows. The first floor of the house elevated us enough to see past the cemetery. In the distance two rivers caused the land to form a deep curve. A railroad bridge crossed one river, and tracks ran along side its left bank. The rooftops of long, narrow buildings lined the other side of the tracks. More gun shots and the distant sound of mob shouts could be heard.

"Let's go see what's shaking," exclaimed Chelsea.

Brad warned, "We're too conspicuous in these clothes. That might be risky."

"Step right this way, folks, into my department store." I gestured toward a back window and a clothesline sagging with dresses, petticoats, and young men's work clothes. "Men's wear on the right, ladies' ready-to-wear on the left. Please use the dressing room down the path."

"All right!" Chelsea laughed. "I want the white dress with the little blue flowers. Brad, the long brown pants and white shirt with buttons will do for you. Oh, for a fashion flare, big brother, you might want to add those red suspenders."

"Yes, ma'am," Brad answered, running out the front door with Chelsea and me right behind him.

I removed the clothespins from a light green dress and held it up. "What do you think, Chelsea?"

"It looks great with your red hair," Chelsea answered, as she pulled the dress with tiny blue flowers over her head.

"Just call me Billy Joe Brad Bob from Virginny, folks," said Brad, as he bowed low, decked out in his brown pants, red suspenders, and white shirt.

"Let's take off these tennis shoes," I suggested. "They're a sure giveaway."

I unlaced my shoes and hid them alongside Chelsea's and Brad's under some loose floorboards in the front porch. My new clothes weren't the best fitting that I ever had, but I could pass a casual inspection. I started barefooted down the winding path through the cemetery to the town below. The path led to a cobblestone road that dropped to the bottom of the hill. Wooden saltbox houses perched above the road on the right, while the roof tops of houses hugging the railroad were visible on the left. The neatly trimmed green lawns were guarded by golden maple, red dogwood, and orange-leafed apple trees. The sound of angry voices, barking dogs, and soldiers shouting commands floated up from the street below. A crowd, mostly of women and children, came into view as we rounded the corner. A yellow dog signaled our approach, as he came rushing and barking toward me.

"Here, boy," Brad said, bending on one knee and slapping his chest.

The dog altered his course and jumped toward Brad. He playfully licked Brad's face and began jumping toward his outstretched hands.

Brad pretended to be playing with the dog, as he studied the scene below. "This looks safe enough," he mumbled. "Let's get our story straight. We don't change our names, got it? We're here to visit our Uncle Josh . . . and . . . eh . . . the wagon wheel broke when we hit this big rock. We've come to town to look for a new wheel. Any questions so far?"

"Yeah," Chelsea began. "Where does Uncle Josh live and do we have an aunt?"

"Uncle Josh lives in Maryland," Brad answered "and our aunt . . . "

"Her name is Sue, Aunt Sue," I interrupted. "That's the truth; the fewer lies the easier to remember."

Brad agreed. "Right. Let's head toward the large woman in the brown and white dress."

Chelsea asked, "Next to the pretty girl dressed in yellow?"

Brad ignored Chelsea and continued, "Remember, I'll do all the talking."

We walked down the hill with the dog running and jumping at our heels. The crowd was so involved in what was happening up the street that no one noticed us.

"Good day, ma'am," Brad said to the woman in the brown and white dress.

The woman turned, half smiled, and said, "Good day."

"Big crowd here today, don't you think so, ma'am?"

Turning slightly around, she answered coldly, "Yes, of course."

"Eh . . . we just got into town. Our wagon broke a wheel, just up the road a piece. Eh . . . do you mind telling me what is going on?" Brad continued.

The young girl in the bright yellow dress turned and smiled. "You mean you all don't know about the hangin'?" she asked.

Brad stammered, "No, ma'am. I . . . we don't. What hanging?"

"John Brown," she explained, "the hangin' is suppose to be at noon, but the cadets aren't here yet. My daddy's the sheriff. He says he's not goin' to start any hangin' till the extra soldiers, those cadets from the military school, get here. Daddy says there may be trouble with all the people comin' into town for the hangin'."

Brad stood smiling at the honey-haired girl and began to explain, "Our wagon broke a wheel . . . "

"I know you all had trouble," she said sweetly. "I heard you explainin' to my momma. My name is Sarah, Sarah Morgan."

"Pleased to meet you, ma'am," said Brad as he kissed her hand. "I'm Brad Brown; this is my sister, Chelsea, and my cousin Ginny Lucas. We're on our way to visit our Uncle Josh and Aunt Sue."

"I'm so glad you all stopped here in Harpers Ferry to visit, I mean to repair that mean old wagon," Sarah sang.

"Gag," Chelsea mumbled, "I think 'we all' just might throw up."

Sarah touched Brad's arm as she leaned toward Chelsea. "I'm sorry, darlin'. Are you ill?"

Chelsea fanned herself with her hand and replied, "Not just yet, but I'm working on it."

"Oh dear, oh dear," sweet Sarah fretted. "You poor thing. Let me help you over yonder to Miss Molly's veranda. I just know Miss Molly can serve you some nice old lemonade."

Sarah put one arm around Chelsea's shoulder, the other around her waist, and began to maneuver her through the crowd toward a yellow saltbox. The two-story house had been converted into a tavern. Additional tables and chairs had been placed on the veranda to accomodate visitors for the hanging. Sarah, after taking great measure to seat Chelsea gently in a chair, smiled and winked at Brad over her shoulder. He acted like a stray dog, panting and following at her heels. I really expected him to jump up and down and bark. I felt invisible again as I stopped in front of the veranda to read the bill of fare. The rapid pop, pop, pop of a rifle made me hop onto the porch and scurry to the table where Brad, Chelsea, and sweet Sarah were seated.

"What's all the shooting about?" I asked.

"Sometimes it's the soldiers tryin' to move the crowd back with warnin' shots. Sometimes it's Mr. Tackett or Widow Tygart tryin' to move moochers off the paid line," Sarah explained, fluttering her long eyelashes at Brad and forgetting I was the one who asked the question.

I continued, "Paid line? What's a paid line?"

"Why, darlin', haven't you ever been to a hangin' before?" Sarah seemed taken back with surprise.

"No, darlin'," I mocked. "It's really not one of my favorite things."

"If you want a really good seat for a hangin', the best place is in front of Mr. Tackett's General Store or the Widow Tygart's Hat Shoppe." Sarah continued, "They set up chairs and rent them for two bits. Sometimes, mean ol' riff raff comes into town and tries to take these good seats without payin'. So the Widow Tygart and Mr. Tackett have no other choice than to shoo them away."

Chelsea with wide eyes gasped and said, "With guns?"

"They just fire them up in the air. Why they wouldn't harm the hair on a flea," giggled sweet Sarah.

"Were you waiting for the hanging?" Brad asked.

Sarah tilted her head and puckered her lips. "Not really. I was on my way with Momma to the market for fresh eggs and butter. Daddy said he would send Josie for us when he was ready to start the hangin'. Momma and I always watch the hangin's from inside the jail. You get a much better view, and people don't step all over your dress and muddy your shoes."

"I sure wouldn't want to muddy my shoes or dirty my dress for a hangin'," I said in a sneering voice.

Ignoring my comments and smiling at Brad, Sarah offered, "If you all want to stay for the hangin', I'm sure my daddy would let you watch with me from the jail."

Brad stammered, "Eh, we hadn't thought about that. Uncle Josh and Aunt Sue are . . . "

Resting her hand on Brad's arm, Sarah said, "The best seats in the house are inside the jail."

"I don't want to see anyone hanged," Chelsea replied firmly.

"Me neither." I frowned.

"Well, my goodness," cooed Sarah, "I was just trying to be hospitable." She removed her hand from Brad's arm and tilted her nose in the air. "You all don't need to sound so miffed."

Brad, reaching for her hand, said, "I'd love to go to the hanging with you." Turning toward Chelsea and me, he said, "You two don't have to go. I can meet you back here later. Is that okay with you, Sis? Ginny?''

Chelsea, looking very disgusted, answered, ''Brad Brown, I can't believe you! You mean you really want to see a man hanged? You want to witness this public display of violence? What would Mom and Dad . . . ''

''Hey,'' remarked Brad angrily, ''I'm old enough to make my own decisions. Anyway, I'm not forcing you or Ginny to go.''

''He's right, Chelsea,'' I said. ''We don't have to go. If he wants to watch, that's his business.''

Sarah's eyes sparkled with victory as she watched Brad argue with Chelsea. Not only would Brad be with her, but she would have him alone.

Our waiter, a ten-year-old black boy, cleared the table and wiped it clean with a damp yellow cloth. With his head bowed, he mumbled, ''Yes'um Miss Sarah.''

''We all would like a tall glass of lemonade,'' sang Sarah, ''and be sure you put in lots of ice.''

Using his left barefoot to scratch his right ankle, he answered without looking up, ''Sor'y, Miss Sarah. Ain't got no mo' leminade. Miss Molly got sum mint tea. Dat's all dat's left.''

Pouting, Sarah said, ''Well, I guess that will have to do. Do you all fancy some mint tea?''

''Pepsi, I want a Pepsi,'' said Chelsea, glaring at Brad.

Sarah asked, ''A what?''

''Never mind her,'' Brad said. He tried his best to kick Chelsea under the table. ''Mint tea sounds just great.''

Sarah nodded toward the young boy. He moved to three more tables and took orders before he disappeared through a swinging door.

''How does he keep all these orders straight?'' I asked. ''He didn't write anything down.''

Sarah gasped, ''Of course not; Toby can't write. Miss Molly isn't about to break any laws. This here is a respectable boardin' house.''

''It's against the law to write?'' I questioned.

A serious look came over Sarah's face. She asked, ''Are you all from up north?''

''We're from south of here,'' Chelsea answered.

Looking somewhat relieved, Sarah remarked, ''Then you should know it's against the law to teach a slave to read or write. Toby's a slave.

My goodness, gracious, there was only one free black in Harpers Ferry, and even he didn't know how to read or write."

"Was? You mean he is no longer free?" asked Brad.

Sarah replied, "He's no longer livin'. Heywood Shepherd was the baggage master at the railroad station. He was killed the night of the raid."

I asked, "John Brown's raid?"

"Was anyone else killed that night?" asked Brad.

"No, not that night," replied Sarah. "Daddy said two of the hostages, the mayor of Harpers Ferry and the station agent, were killed the next day when the marines stormed the fort. And I believe . . . Daddy said two or three of Brown's raiders were killed."

I remembered the newspaper article, so I asked, "What happened to Washington's sword and his nephew?"

"You must mean his great-grandnephew, Col. Lewis Washington," Sarah answered. "He and the sword were rescued. Daddy said he saw John Brown when he rode into town waving that sword. Daddy said he looked like a madman. His white hair and long beard were uncombed, standing on end, and his eyes were glazed and wild-looking. He had his Bible tucked under his arm, and he quoted scripture aloud as his men went into the arsenal. It's a good thing the militia from Charles Town surrounded that arsenal. They kept Brown and his raiders from escaping until the marines arrived."

"Are the marines still here?" asked Brad.

"Only a few," Sarah began. "That's why Daddy is waiting for the cadets from Virginia Military Institute to get here. There's been rumors all week that Northerners might come down and try to rescue John Brown. Some Yankees think he's a hero. All the menfolk around here strapped on their guns, just in case anyone tried to save that slave lover. Daddy says . . ."

"They're here. Let's go. Bring him out . . ." shouted ominous voices from somewhere down the street.

The patrons began to leave the veranda and file into the front yard. The milling crowd, standing at the bottom of the hill, made way for three men on horseback and a double line of the Virginia Military Institute cadets to pass. The cadets were dressed in grey pants with plain, dark blue jackets. The brass buttons on the jackets formed two rows from the waist to the turned-up collars. Their dark blue caps with black chin straps, were pulled low to shade their eyes. They carried rifles strapped over

66

their shoulders and canteens attached to their belts. They kept their eyes fastened on the three horsemen in front of the regiment, as they stepped to the best of a drum. The lead horseman, dressed like the cadets, carried the United States flag. The two horsemen behind him were dressed in dark blue uniforms. The younger man's uniform had the traditional double row of brass buttons plus a lone medal pinned on his chest. The older man's uniform was embellished with gold cords and the insignia of a lieutenant colonel. This dark, bearded man rode straight-backed and determined toward the gallows at the end of the street. The crowd closed in behind the last two cadets, as mothers gathered small children to take them home.

"Professor, Professor Jackson," shouted a well-dressed man holding a pad and pencil. "Could I have a word with you, sir?" he asked, running alongside the bearded officer's horse. "How many cadets have you brought with you?"

The lieutenant colonel ignored the questions. He kept his horse moving at an easy gait and in a straight line.

"Are you expecting any trouble today?" the man shouted, trying to get the officer's attention. "Please, sir, just a few words for my newspaper?"

The contingent of men moved to the end of the street. When the officer raised his hand, they stopped. He dismounted and tied his horse to the hitching post in front of the jail. The younger man with the medal shouted a few commands, and the cadets formed a single square around the gallows. The lieutenant colonel walked slowly inside the square facing the young cadets. He then nodded solemnly and entered the jail.

The menacing crowd began to cheer and rush toward the end of the street. Shouts of "I'll pull the rope," "Let's get rid of that troublemaker," "He's a thief, tryin' to free my slaves and, givin' them guns," "wanted us all dead," filled the air.

Sarah put her hand on Brad's arm and said, "We'd better hurry to the jail. The hangin' should begin just real soon now."

"Sarah," swallowed Brad, "I've changed my mind. I don't think I want to watch."

"I offered you the best seat in the house and you have the nerve to stand me up. Well, I never," stormed Sarah. She stomped down the street, leaving us alone.

We joined the lone reporter standing in the street. He was busily writing notes on his pad. He looked up, nodded toward us, and finished scribbling a few words.

"You folks had better hurry or you'll miss the big event," the reporter commented flatly.

"No, thanks," Brad replied. "That's not for us."

"Did you call that officer, Professor?" I questioned.

"Yes, little lady. That was Prof. Thomas Jackson; he teaches at Virginia Military Institute in Lexington, Virginia. Tommy and I grew up together in Greenbrier County. I though he would at least answer my questions. I had hoped for an interview, but Tommy was never much of a talker," offered the reporter.

Brad bristled with excitement when he said, "You mean that was 'Stonewall' Jackson?"

"No, son," the confused reporter replied, "Thomas Jonathan Jackson. I've never heard of a 'Stonewall' Jackson. I knew of a Sonny Jackson once."

Brad's eyes widened when he suggested, "Maybe we should go down. Just for a closer look. What do you say, Chelsea? Ginny? We'll leave before the hanging."

"You folks do what you want," the reporter remarked. "I've seen too many of these." He finished his notes, put the pad and pencil in his coat pocket, turned and walked toward the hill away from the crowd.

I demanded, "Brad, why? Why did you change your mind?"

"Didn't you hear him, Ginny?" Brad asked. "He said Professor Thomas Jackson! In just a few years he will be known as 'Stonewall' Jackson, one of the greatest Confederate generals in the Civil War. Can you imagine? A chance to see 'Stonewall' Jackson."

Chelsea asked, "If we go with you, will you leave before the hanging?"

"Yes," Brad promised. "Hey, all I want to do is get a good look at 'Stonewall' Jackson."

I nodded toward Chelsea and answered, "Okay."

The three of us started down the street toward the crowd. The cross bars of the scaffold with three dangling nooses could be seen above the crowd. A man, standing on top of the stage, placed a large sandbag under the middle noose and signaled with his arm. The sandbag disappeared with a thud, and the crowd cheered.

Brad paused and commented, "Maybe the two of you should wait here. I don't know what this crowd might do. It may get ugly."

68

"Not if we leave before they hang the man," I said.

Chelsea remarked, "I'd rather we stick together."

"Okay," Brad agreed, "but if anything happens and we get separated, go back to the brick house above the cemetery. That will be our meeting place."

Brad positioned himself in front of Chelsea and me as we neared the outer edge of the crowd. A few stragglers with solemn expressions talked softly to one another. As we edged by these men into the middle of the crowd, we found a mixture of older men and women talking excitedly about the hanging. We elbowed our way to the front, where mostly women were gathered. They were shaking their fists, waving their arms,and yelling for the hanging to start. The young cadets, with fear in their eyes and a look of bewilderment on their faces, stared nervously at the restless mob.

Brad pushed his way to the front line and made room for Chelsea and me. He leaned against the single rope barrier that separated the young cadets from the onlookers.

"Do not pass the rope, sir," ordered a cadet to Brad.

Brad asked, "Has Professor Jackson come out of the jail, yet?"

"No, sir," answered the cadet, who appeared to be the same age as Brad. "Sir, you need to move back. We must keep the rope tight for security."

"Do you have classes with Professor Jackson?" Brad probed the cadet.

The cadet put aside his military behavior and answered, "Yes, sir, I do. I have military tactics with Mr. Jackson."

"That's fantastic," Brad replied. "I bet he's great."

The young soldier grinned and looked out of the corner of his eye to see if his commanding officer was watching. "It's awful. He memorizes his notes, and his lectures last for hours. He . . . "

"Booth, Cadet John Booth," called an angry voice. "Must you be reminded you are on duty?"

"Yes, sir," snapped Cadet Booth. He stiffened his stance and faced straight ahead.

"You wouldn't be John Wilkes Booth, would you?" I gasped.

Only the cadet's eyes moved as he forced himself to stay at attention. He kept trying to see who asked the question.

When the commanding officer turned to scold another cadet, John Wilkes Booth replied, "Yes, I am. Do I know you?"

69

"You're really John Wilkes Booth?" I whispered and held my breath.

"Yes," he answered anxiously. "I beg your pardon, ma'am. Have we met before?"

"Chelsea, Brad," I stammered, "Did you hear that? He's . . . could it really be the John Wilkes Booth that killed Abraham Lincoln?"

"There's one way to find out," Brad mumbled. When the officer in charge moved toward the gallows and away from Cadet Booth, Brad asked in a low voice, "Is your brother, Edwin Booth, the Shakespearean actor?"

This last question caught the young soldier off guard. He relaxed his stance and turned his head to face Brad. "Yes, how do you know me?" he answered, trying to recognize this stranger.

The expression on Brad's face changed from amazement to hostility. He jumped over the rope barrier and grabbed the cadet by the neck. Booth dropped his rifle and tried to loosen Brad's grip. Three soldiers, after dropping the rope barrier, rushed to Booth's aid and wrestled Brad to the ground. The throng, anxious to see a fight, formed a circle around the young men. The commanding officer broke through the crowd and pulled Booth to his feet.

"Why this disorderly conduct, Cadet Booth?" shouted the officer.

"Sir, the man attacked me," panted Booth.

The officer loosened his hold on Booth and faced Brad. "Do you realize it is against the law to provoke a soldier while on duty?"

"You don't understand," Brad responded eagerly. "That's John Wilkes Booth. He's going to . . . " Brad stopped. He looked at Chelsea and me. He realized no one would possibly believe what he was going to say.

"Take him to the guardhouse. Wait, take them both," commanded the officer. "Booth, this is your last infraction. Don't you realize we are here to keep law and order? Instead, you get into a fight with a civilian."

Chelsea reached for the officer's arm and began to beg, "Wait, please wait. That's my brother and he hasn't been well. My cousin and I were taking him to our uncle's house when our wagon . . . "

The officer interrupted firmly, "I'm sorry, ma'am. We'll need to hold your brother in the guardhouse until the hanging is over. If you speak to Lieutenant Colonel Jackson later today, he may decide to release him."

The officer signaled for two soldiers to come forward. "Take them to the guardhouse. Hold them until further notice."

He turned abruptly and began shouting orders to the cadets. The remaining soldiers busied themselves with quieting the crowd and raising the rope barrier. Brad and Booth, with raised arms and hands folded behind their heads, walked between two armed guards toward an old log cabin used as a military jail. They disappeared inside, without looking back.

"What will we do now?" Chelsea said, tears staining her face.

I suggested, "Let's get out of this mess and check out that guardhouse."

I took Chelsea's arm and led her through the crowd that was forming again near the rope barrier. The town jail door opened as the crowd cheered and surged forward. I was shoved to my knees as a large woman bolted between Chelsea and me.

"I'll pull the rope," she offered, trying to get past the cadets.

I regained my footing and pulled Chelsea out of the throng. No one noticed as we skirted the edge of the mob to reach the guardhouse. One guard stood at attention in front of the door. The other guard climbed atop the hitching post to see what was happening when shouts and cheers from the mob grew louder and louder.

The guard on the hitching post jumped down, said a few words to the lone soldier in front of the door, and disappeared into the mob. Chelsea and I walked within four feet of the remaining guard and stopped.

"I'm Ginny Lucas and this is Chelsea Brown," I began. "The civilian just taken prisoner is a relative of ours. Could we see him, please?"

"Beat it," growled the guard. "This is no place for nosey girls."

Chelsea begged, "Could I just talk to him for a moment? To see if he's all right?"

"Look," snapped the soldier, "I said to beat it. You two tryin' to get me in trouble?"

"Please, sir, he was taking us to our uncle's house. Now we are alone and don't know how to get there. We don't even know how to reach Uncle Josh. Couldn't we just talk to him?" I pleaded.

The guard's eyes swept the area and his gaze settled on us. He sighed and said, "There is a window out back. You can talk to him through the window. If you get caught, I'll swear I didn't know you were there. Now make it snappy."

71

Chelsea and I hurried around to the back of the log house. A tree stump had been placed underneath the barred window, a remnant of past visits. It was roomy enough to hold us both, as we reached for the bars and strained to see Brad.

Chelsea whispered through the bars, "Brad, Brad? Are you okay?"

Brad's face became visible through the bars. "Chelsea, Ginny, you shouldn't be here. I told you if anything happened we would meet at the old house."

"Fat chance," I muttered. "We've got to get you out of here first."

"I can't believe you can act so dumb, Brad Brown! What made you attack that cadet?" asked Chelsea.

Brad answered angrily, "Didn't you realize who he was? You heard him, Chelsea. That was John Wilkes Booth. I could have saved . . . "

Chelsea snapped back, "You can't change history, remember?"

Brad dropped his eyes and moved from the window. He reappeared and mumbled, "You're right, I really made a mess of things. I'm sorry I got you two into this, but . . . "

I interrupted, "Let's leave now. Here's the horseshoe . . . . "

The loud cheering and applause from the street area suddenly stopped. The air seemed to hang heavy with anticipation and silence. After a few seconds a man's voice could be heard. The calm voice grew louder and started to tremble. It softened and then boomed the phrase "with God as my keeper . . . " Snap. Thump. Screams, shouts, moans, gun shots, and cheers clashed and echoed between the hills. It sounded like a wild party had started.

"It's too dark in here. You keep it," said Brad.

Chelsea began, "Hold it up now, Ginny. If you turn toward that maple tree and catch those beams, it may work."

As I turned with the horseshoe in my hand, I caught a glimpse of the guard rounding the side of the house. I dropped my arm quickly and tightened my fist around the golden horseshoe.

The corners of the guard's mouth turned upward when he asked, "What's that shiny thing you holdin', miss? You wouldn't be holdin' a twenty dollar gold piece, would you?"

"I . . . I don't know w-what you mean?" I lied.

"Now you either show me what you have in your hand or that relative of yours might get shot for jail breakin'. What's it goin' to be, little lady?"

"It's really nothing special," I mumbled. "Just an old fake pendant that belonged to my grandma."

The guard sneered as he nudged my clenched fist with the barrel of his rifle. "Let's see what kind of taste the old lady has. Hand it here."

"You leave her alone," Chelsea ordered, jumping down from the stump.

The guard moved closer and threatened, "Give me that pendant or I'll blow your head off right now!"

"Eeeiiii!!!" screamed Chelsea.

"That mob out front can't hear you. Ain't nobody goin' help you gals," chuckled the guard.

He yanked me from the stump and gripped my wrist. I felt an agonizing pain shoot up my arm as my fingers opened and the horseshoe fell to the ground. The butt of his rifle met my cheek and knocked me against the side of the log cabin. Chelsea darted to grab the horseshoe but a kick from the guard left her sprawled in the dirt. As she struggled to her knees, the soldier slapped her across the face.

"Take it. You can have it," I cried, falling to my knees and holding my dangling arm. "Please, just leave us alone."

The guard smiled as he spit on the golden horseshoe to wipe it off. He lowered the gun to his side as he studied the precious stones. He pulled a pen knife from his pocket and began to prick the stones from the gold.

Brad, who had been screaming threats at the guard during the shuffle, called to us, "Chelsea, Ginny, one of you, go for help! Hurry!"

"Just hold it, right there," said the guard as he picked up his gun." He motioned with his rifle for Chelsea to move over to the cabin beside me.

"What's going on here, Private James?" questioned a large uniformed man standing at the far corner of the guardhouse.

The guard jumped to attention and answered, "Nothing, sir. I caught them little gals here talkin' to that civilian troublemaker. The one that jumped on Cadet Booth."

"He has my grandmother's pendant," I blurted out. "He took it away from me."

Chelsea whimpered, "He kicked and slapped me. He hit Ginny with his rifle."

"No, sir," lied the guard. "Those girls attacked me when I ordered them to get down from the window. They were talkin' to that new prisoner about a breakout.

"That's a lie!" Brad shouted from inside the jail.

I said, "That's not true. We weren't planning any breakout. We said we . . . "

Chelsea interrupted, "He's a liar. He stole our horseshoe and . . . "

The officer held up his hand, and everyone became silent. "I can see this is going to take some time," he began. "Private James, return the pendant to the young ladies and report to camp headquarters. Ladies, we will hold a hearing after supper tonight and discuss your charges against Private James. I will need to have you report back here at nineteen hundred hours."

"But what about my brother?" Chelsea asked.

"The young man who provoked Cadet Booth?" the officer questioned.

Chelsea nodded and explained, "He's been ill, sir. I think it's a real bad disease. In fact, if we don't get him out of here soon, everyone in this town could die."

The officer smiled and responded, "We'll discuss your ill brother at nineteen hundred hours also. Private James, the pendant."

The private shoved the horseshoe in my hand and stepped on my toes as he trudged past. He kicked at the dirt and mumbled under his breath when he walked past Charles. He tossed his rifle to the officer and disappeared around the corner of the log guardhouse.

Chelsea and I dashed for the stump. I held the horseshoe up to catch the light, I gasped, "He took some of the stones. That rotten thief."

"Tell the officer tonight at the hearing," Brad suggested.

"Let me see," Chelsea demanded, looking at the golden horseshoe. She continued, "All the sapphires are missing. There are only two diamonds left."

"We'll get them back," Brad promised.

"I really don't care if we do or not," I said. "I'm ready to leave, aren't you?"

"But, Ginny," Chelsea continued, "what if we've lost too many gems? What if it the horseshoe won't work now?"

Brad responded, "I'm with Ginny. I'm ready to go, Chelsea. Let's give it another try."

"Okay, you talked me into it," Chelsea finally agreed. "Shouldn't we get rid of these fancy country rags before we split?"

"That wouldn't be a bad idea," I replied.

Chelsea and I slipped out of our petticoats and dresses, rolled them into two tight bundles and stuffed them between the tree stump and the guardhouse. Brad removed his outer layer of clothes and hid them under the straw tick on the metal bunk.

Chelsea blurted out, "What about our shoes?"

"Forget them," Brad and I answered simultaneously.

"Oh, I guess Mom won't notice we're missing our shoes when we get home," Chelsea began. "Or, what if we don't get home? What if we . . . "

"Would you just shut up with the 'what ifs' and get over here?" insisted Brad.

"Hey, don't you yell at me, big brother. Remember, I'm out here with the golden horseshoe. Besides, Ginny and I haven't decided if we want you along or not," teased Chelsea.

Chelsea joined me on the stump, and Brad stood patiently on his side of the window. I held the horseshoe up to the light turning the last two diamonds upward. The sun danced on the stones as they sparkled radiantly. I turned the horseshoe slowly back and forth. At times the light was blinding, but then it faded.

I worried aloud, "Maybe Chelsea was right. We must need the missing sapphires. What if we can't get them back from Private James?"

"It's my stupid fault," stated Brad. "It's because I'm in this jail. I'm sorry. I guess we'll have to wait until I get out of here."

"Hello-o-o you all," sang a familiar voice rounding the corner of the guardhouse and heading toward us. "Wasn't it excitin', you know, the hangin' and all? I heard Brad caused some excitement too, when . . . "

Chelsea grabbed the horseshoe and held it in front of the metal bars. A flash of light crossed from the gold to the steel. She turned the horseshoe frantically as the flashes grew brighter.

"Come on, come on," I mumbled. "Please . . . "

It was working. The light was glowing brighter and bigger. There it was. The blazing red flash, the blinding white light, and the simmering rich amber all began to swirl overhead. The swirling changed into a spiral, but no horseshoe appeared. When I reached out to find the horseshoe, I began to fall. Down. Down. I was free falling through a red and amber tunnel into a brilliant white sea. S-P-L-A-S-H!

75

Facts

1. On October 16, 1859, John Brown led a surprise attack on Harpers Ferry to capture the arsenal and rifle works.
2. John Brown carried a Bible and the stolen sword of George Washington when he entered the town.
2. Col. Lewis W. Washington, great-grandnephew of George Washington, was held hostage by John Brown and his raiders.
4. The United States Marines, under the command of Col. Robert E. Lee and Lt. J. E. B. Stuart, seized Brown and some of his men who had taken refuge in the engine house on October 18. 1859.
5. John Brown was arrested and stood trial in nearby Charles Town.
6. On December 2, 1859, John Brown was hanged in Charles Town.
7. Local authorities, afraid of violent outbreaks on that day, requested additional militiamen to protect the city. A corps of cadets from Virginia Military Institute under the command of Thomas Jonathan (known as "Stonewall" after the Battle of Bull Run) Jackson was dispatched to Charles Town.
8 When John Brown fell to his death, Cadet John Wilkes Booth fainted. The commanding officer, Thomas Jackson, helped the future assassin of Abraham Lincoln to his feet.

Main road leading into Harpers Ferry.

View of the housetops from the cemetery path into town.

John Brown's fort at Harpers Ferry.

Thomas "Stonewall" Jackson, the commander of the corps of cadets from Virginia Military Institute, was dispatched to keep order during the hanging of John Brown.

Chapter 6

The Hatfield-McCoy Feud

I splashed into cool, white shimmering light. I opened my eyes and gasped for breath; the light was drowning me. Suddenly I realized I was under water, not light. I thrashed with my arms and legs to push upward toward the surface. Just when I thought my lungs would burst, my head broke through icy cold water. I panted and gulped in the fresh air while I wiped my eyes. I treaded water as I looked about for Chelsea and Brad. They were nowhere in sight. As I swam to shore I decided this must be a creek and not a river, since it was deep in the middle and not very wide. I waded onto the sloping creek bank and leaned against the trunk of a papaw tree to rest.

I called softly, "Chelsea, Brad, where are you?" then louder, "Chelsea, Brad, can you hear me? I'm over here?"

Only the rippling creek, a few chirping birds and the hum from a swarm of bees answered. I studied my surroundings. The trees and plants looked familiar. Maybe I was on the hill behind Grandma's house. What if . . . I bet the horseshoe worked this time! Chelsea and Brad were probably already at Grandma's waiting for me. I bet this was the same creek that flowed behind her house. All I had to do was follow it. I jumped to my feet and ouch—something cut into my foot. Under my dripping jeans and bare feet lay the horseshoe. I picked it up and tried to wipe it clean with the tail of my wet T-shirt. I stuck the horseshoe in my pocket and decided to walk downstream with the flow of the creek. I walked near the water's edge in the soft mud and called for Brad and Chelsea from time to time.

"Young'un, you stop right there. Who do you belong to and what you a doin' here on Blackberry Creek?" asked a raspy voice as a gun barrel pressed against my back.

I started to turn and stammered. "I . . . I was l-look . . . "

"Did I tell you to turn around?" questioned the husky female voice, as the gun pushed deeper into my back.

"N-no, ma'am," I muttered.

"Put your hands up," she demanded, as she patted my pockets to see if I carried a gun. "Now you turn around real slow like and recollect you are to keep your hands in the air."

I turned slowly and found myself facing a middle-aged woman of average build. Her gray-streaked brown hair was piled high on top of her head with only a few wisps around her face. The high-collared, long sleeved black blouse was unbuttoned at the neck and the sleeves were rolled to her elbows. Her long black skirt, so as not to get wet or muddy, was folded above her knees and tucked in at the waist. She held a burlap bag in her right hand and a long walking stick in the left. The end of the raised stick was the "gun" that pushed into my back.

She held the stick in a threatening position as she continued to question me. "Maybe you didn't hear me, young-un. I asked your name and your business on Blackberry Creek?"

"I-I-I'm Ginny Lucas and I-I'm looking for my cousins, Chelsea and Brad Brown," I managed to whisper.

"Ain't never heard of any Lucases or Browns in these here parts," she said in a piercing voice. "You got any kin from across Tug River?"

"I . . . I don't know. I'm not sure what you m-mean," I stammered.

The woman became angry and jabbed my shoulder with the stick. "Don't play games with me. You know what I mean. You any kin to Anse Hatfield? Ellison Hatfield? You wouldn't be Ellison's oldest girl, now would you?"

"No," I blurted, "honest, I'm not related to any Hatfields. My name is Ginny Lucas, and I'm looking for my cousins. That's the truth. I swear."

The woman studied me carefully and lowered the stick. "How'd you get here?" she asked.

Her manner of dress and speech let me know the horseshoe had not brought me home. I had no idea where I was or in what time period. I remembered a story I had read about an abused child, so I decided to try that. "I ran away from home," I lied. "I was staying with my Uncle Ron and Aunt Fran, and I got tired of the beatings. I left. My cousins, who were also beaten and starved, left too. We were following this creek to find my cousins' friend. This morning, when I woke up, my cousins were gone.''

"Sounds strange to me. Your kin just a leavin' you here in the woods," she remarked with that eerie stare.

"W-we didn't have much food," I continued. "I guess they thought their chances were better for survival without me."

"I don't believe your story, but I'll let Cal decide. You look like one of them Hatfield women to me. They never did dress like ladies," she commented looking at my jeans.

"You've got to believe me," I begged. "I don't know any Hatfields."

She chuckled, "You spies are all alike. You make them lies seem convincin'. Here young'un," she said shoving the burlap sack toward me, "you carry this poke while I finish my gathering. Then we'll go back to the homeplace and see what my kinfolk think about your tale of woe."

I shifted the gathered neck of the lightweight burlap bag into my right hand and muttered, "Yes, ma'am."

"Up here," she called moving away from the river bank toward some dogwood trees.

I followed her to the trees and watched, while she picked the red berries and stripped the bark from the trunk. She gestured for me to open the sack.

"Did you call that creek Blackberry Creek?" I asked.

"That I did," she answered, as she dumped the berries and bark into the sack.

"Just where is this creek in West Virginia?" I continued to question.

She laughed and replied, "You are one of the best spies them Hatfields ever sent. Young-un, I wish you were on our side."

I was getting very frustrated because this woman wouldn't believe me. "Please tell me where I am," I asked with tears in my eyes.

The woman noticed my tears. "Young-un, you're telling me the truth, aren't you?"

I nodded and wiped my eyes. "I need to know who you are. And where am I? I need to find my cousins, Chelsea and Brad." I began to cry softly.

The woman hugged me warmly and took the bag from my hand. She seated me on a large flat rock and patted my knee. "Young'un, you're on Blackberry Creek in Kentucky. West Virginia is right over yonder, 'bout three-hundred feet 'cross the Tug River. I'm Sadie McCoy.

81

My kin, my pa and brothers, they bin fightin' the Hatfields since the Civil War. Ever since my Uncle Harmon, he was for the Union, was kilt by them Hatfields.''

I nodded and wiped my eyes with the back of my hand. "I heard about a feud between your families. I don't want to get involved with any fighting or killing. If I could just find my cousins, we'll leave," I promised.

Sadie remarked, "Ginny, I followed Blackberry Creek from its head to the Tug this morning. I ain't seen hide or hair of any other livin' bein' except you.''

"Are you sure?" I asked, hoping her answer would change.

She answered firmly, "As sure as a tick on a dog's back. Now, I need to gather some roots and berries, a little basil, and maybe pull down some mistletoe. All them things I need for my cures. Ain't got no real doctors out here. When my kin get to ailin', they depend on me to make 'em feel better.''

I nodded as Sadie patted my hand and continued, "This here holler ain't fittin' place for a young'un all alone. I think it best that you help me fetch my cures and then come on home with me. I'll talk to Cal and see if he can find out anything about your kin.''

I nodded and took a deep breath. My body felt numb with confusion, while my mind whirled with questions. What would I do if I couldn't find Chelsea or Brad? If I tried the horseshoe would I return to Harpers Ferry? Would I be sent home? Where were Chelsea and Brad? What if I never saw them again? I panicked. I couldn't seem to breathe. I began to sob uncontrollably.

Sadie put both arms around me and said softly, "Ginny, Ginny, nothin' in the world could be that bad. Young'un, you just plan to stay with Aunt Sadie for a spell. We'll find those long lost cousins. Child, just quit your frettin', it's goin' be all right.''

I wiped my eyes with my fists and sighed, "I guess I'd better help you find those cures.''

"That's right, young'un," Sadie answered cheerfully, as she hopped up from the rock. "We need to dig some sassafras and ginseng, them make mighty powerful tonics. And I need to get more dogwood and juniper berries. Aunt Tildy really fancies that juniper berry tea. She swears it helps her kidneys. The menfolk say them dogwood berries help with the malaria. They picked up that malaria fightin' against them Johnny Rebs down south.''

"What's in the bag?" I asked, trying to make my mind focus on Sadie and her medicines instead of my troubles.

"Young'un," Sadie began, "I got some of the finest May apple roots and rhododendron roots for poultice that you've ever seen."

"A pol-what?" I asked.

"Poultice, young'un, a poultice," Sadie explained. "Ain't you ever been bit by a snake or got the Saint Anthony's fire? You grind up them roots, mix 'em with just a little boiling water, and then you spread that mixture on the poisoned spot. Now that poultice, that's the mixture child, will draw out any poison or infection. Who does the doctorin' at your house?"

"Oh, we're pretty healthy where I'm from. We've never needed a doctor or a poultice," I assured her.

Sadie leaned forward and asked, "Pretty hearty, you say. Does that aunt of yours believe in them asafetida bags?"

"Is that anything like a tote bag or a litter bag?" I responded.

Sadie, completely confused, remarked, "Young'un, did you hit your head on the rocks in that creek?"

I replied, "No, ma'am."

"Then what in tarnation is a tote bag and a litter bag? Do you tie 'em around your neck so you won't get the croup?" an exasperated Sadie asked.

Without thinking I blurted out, "We use a vaporizer for croup or just take antihistamines." The look on Sadie's face told me I had said the wrong thing.

Sadie picked up her stick and backed away from me. "You a witch, ain't you? I should have known, just appearing from nowhere."

"No! No, I'm not!" I exclaimed.

"Young'un, I ain't touched a hair on your head. I don't deserve no black magic," said Sadie.

I had to think fast. Sadie kept backing away from me. I remembered her comment about some weird kind of bag. "We do use those bags around our necks for croup. The other things too, but mostly the bags."

Sadie asked in a doubting voice, "What do you put in you asafetida bags?"

I responded, "The same old things everyone uses. Uh, I use some strong roots . . . and eh, sometimes berries."

"Ain't never used any roots or berries in my asafetida bags. Don't you use garlic? Maybe some ramps in the spring?" Sadie questioned.

"Yes, always garlic. I can't believe I forgot that," I lied.

"You hang 'em on all the young'uns?" she continued.

"Uh, I do it just like you do," I commented. "Sadie, I think you could teach me a lot about doctorin'. You sound like you are really up on things."

"I know a little about doctorin', but I don't cast no spells," she said keeping a good distance between us. "If you are a witch I hope you're a white one. That black magic is a turrible thing. It makes the cows go dry and the hens won't lay."

"Please believe me, Sadie," I pleaded. "I'm not a witch. Can we go now, up to your homeplace? You said something earlier about a fellow named Cal who might be able to help me find my cousins."

"Cal's my brother," Sadie replied proudly. "He does all the fightin' and takin' care of the clan since our daddy got kilt. If anyone unusual has showed up on either side of the Tug River, Cal will know it."

"H-he wouldn't kill them, would he?" I asked.

"No, young'un," responded Sadie. "Cal ain't never kilt any living creature, unlessin' he had a good reason. Don't matter what them Hatfields a sayin'; we McCoys are good people. We just want to be left alone."

Sadie handed me the burlap bag. She used her stick to help lift herself from the low rock where she was sitting. I heeded her signal, stood and followed her down a narrow path toward a sinkhole near the creek bed.

As she passed the sinkhole, she pointed and remarked casually, "Yonder's where we throw our sheep-killing dogs."

"S-sheep killing dogs?" I sputtered.

"Young-un," she replied, "you really vex me. Anybody a livin' knows you can't let dogs kill your sheep. We throw them killin' dogs in that sinkhole, and the creek, when it's a floodin', jest washes them away."

Sadie peered out of the corner of her eye and began to move away from me. I knew she was thinking that witch stuff again.

"Oh, I thought you said sleep-killing dogs," I lied. "I just couldn't imagine people as kind as the McCoys killing dogs because they couldn't sleep."

Sadie accepted my explanation and smiled. We continued along the creek bank until we reached a clump of chestnut trees. Sadie picked about a dozen leaves for me to put in the sack.

I asked, "What are these used for, Sadie?"

"Them chestnut leaves make the best tea God's little children ever drank for the whooping cough. They surely do. Now let's cut over this hill to the cherry orchard," she directed.

I followed Sadie to the top of a small hill and looked down on a narrow v-shaped valley. A clump of cherry trees nestled in the vee at the bottom of the hill. Sadie paused from time to time to pick daisies and dandelions, as she side-stepped down the hill.

"I know what those are for," I announced proudly. "They're for wine."

Sadie, very pleased, replied, "That's right, young'un; maybe you didn't bang your head on them rocks. Mmmmm, that wine is the best spring tonic a body could ever drink. Why it cures the rheumatism bettern' red flannel, hot rocks or warm bear grease. Young'un, let me tell you a secret."

Sadie motioned for me to lean close. Squeezing the stems of the dandelion plants, she whispered, "This here juice will remove warts faster than lightnin' can strike a tall oak. I've never known it to fail, child."

I stored the dandelions and daisies in the sack and followed Sadie to the cluster of cherry trees. She stripped some bark from each tree and dug several pieces of root. As I put these in the sack, Sadie removed a piece of cheesecloth from her shirt pocket. She unrolled the cloth, removed a lock of brown hair, and placed the hair in the trunk of a cherry tree.

Noting my surprised expression, Sadie explained, "That's for a little Johnse. His asthma will be better 'fore the little fellar sets down to supper."

Sadie reached for the burlap bag, peered inside, and took a quick inventory. She nodded her head and appeared pleased as she handed me the bag.

"I reckon we can be gittin' back home. Young'un, we did a right smart bit of collectin' today," she announced.

"Fine with me," I agreed. I liked Sadie. She seemed to be simple and caring. It was hard to believe she belonged to a feuding clan. As we climbed back up the hill and trudged along the top of the ridge, I kept watching for signs of Brad and Chelsea. I was afraid to call their names, but I spoke loudly to Sadie in case they were close enough to hear me.

Sadie stopped to look at a nest of yellow jackets under a flat rock.

Next she examined an anthill near a fallen pine tree. She looked away from the ridge, back toward the creek. In a serious tone she asked, "Young'un, did you see those signs?"

I panicked. What signs? What was she talking about? I tried to play it cool when I answered, "Well, not all of them? Which ones did you see?"

Sadie shook her head and muttered, "Young'uns today jest don't see what the good Lord puts right in front of them. That nest of yellow jackets was a sittin' right on the ground and that thar anthill was higher than a hound dog. I guess you didn't see all them blackberry blooms or the dogwood berries either?"

"I saw the blooms and the dogwood berries," I blurted out.

"Well, young'un," Sadie demanded, "what's that a tellin' you?"

"Eh, eh, there will be lots of blackberries and dogwood berries. So . . . so we can get rid of malaria," I proudly proclaimed.

Sadie's face fell, and she shook her head. "No, young'un, it means next winter is gonna be bad, real bad. I don't know what your generation is gonna do without anybody to doctor and read the signs."

Sadie turned and continued her trek across the ridge with me close behind. She stopped dead in her tracks and held her finger to her lips. I sensed danger and realized she wanted me to be still. I listened for gunshots or wild animal sounds. Nothing but squirrels chattering and birds chirping filtered through the air. Afraid to move a muscle or turn my head, I let my eyes dart from side-to-side. In a small clearing to the right of the path, sticks, straw, and cornshucks covered the ground. Sadie pointed with her walking stick toward the clearing and signaled for us to leave the path and swing wide. I followed Sadie as quietly as possible through poison ivy, hawthorne bushes,and moss-covered rocks. About two hundred feet later, she sat down on a fallen trunk to rest.

"What sign did I miss?" I whispered.

Sadie chuckled, "Young'un, that was a bed for some wild hogs. Ain't nary sign gonna tell you about a wild hog. You jest gotta keep your eyes open."

"Are they very dangerous?" I asked.

"Young'un," Sadie answered, "I seen one lad gored to death by a bunch of wild hogs. I ain't fixin' to stand around and watch another."

I gulped and muttered, "Oh."

Sadie slapped her knees with both hands and stood up. "That's enuff restin'. Homeplace is right over yonder hill," she said pointing to the top of the ridge.

Once again we climbed to the top of the ridge and into another v-shaped valley. Wedged between two steep hills was a small, wooden house with a narrow front porch. Thin smoke curled from the stone chimney, and the tin roof glared in the sunlight. The house, plus an outhouse, small, unpainted barn,and a drying shed for tobacco were surrounded by a split rail fence. The enclosed land was a combination vegetable garden, yard, and pasture. One lone cow grazed near the rail fence, while two dogs tried to lap water from the pump near the front porch. A white, spotted horse swished flies from his back as he chomped the grass near the garden. The sound of a chopping axe echoed between the hills.

"Cal!" shouted Sadie. "Cal!"

"Yo, Sadie, down here," The chopping sounds stopped, as a man stepped out from behind the barn and waved.

"I got me a visitor!" Sadie called without moving into the open.

"Send him out," Cal ordered as he laid down his axe, disappeared behind the barn, and returned with a gun.

"It's a she visitor. Now you behave yourself, Cal. This is just a young'un," Sadie warned.

"You gonna send her out or em I gonna half to come after her?" Cal threatened as he raised the shotgun to his shoulder.

"I'm a comin' down with her. And, big brother, we're gonna be mighty close together. You just keep your itchy finger off of that trigger," Sadie ordered.

"Maybe you should go down first and talk to your brother," I suggested.

"Don't pay no attention to Cal. He's just natually suspicious. He acts like that to all strangers," Sadie explained.

Sadie placed the burlap bag in her right hand and put her left hand under my elbow to guide me down the hill. Once we reached the bottom and came inside the fence, Cal lowered the gun to his waist.

Cal, tall and thin with curly red hair and deep blue eyes, welcomed me by spitting tobacco juice at my bare feet. He was dressed like Paul Bunyan—brown laced boots, faded jeans, wide leather belt with a big silver buckle, and no outer shirt. His long red woolen underwear served as a shirt. I felt his eyes burning holes through me as he spit a second time at my feet.

"Cal," Sadie scolded, " 'tain't no way to treat a visitor. Has Ellie started supper yet?"

"Sadie, you'd pick up anything wanderin' in the woods," Cal whispered, thinking I couldn't hear him. "I'm tellin' you for the last time don't be a talkin' to any strangers."

Sadie snapped back, "You don't tell me what to do, Cal McCoy. You ain't my pa, remember. This here young'un was a roamin' lost. Her kin, some no good cousins, went off and left her. You wouldn't want any young'un of yourn out in these woods, would you? I know you wouldn't. So I jest up and brung her home with me."

"She might jest be a Hatfield, Sadie. Ellison's girl ought to be about her age," suggested Cal.

"You must think I got bat brains. She ain't no Hatfield. Do you think I'm dumb enuff to fetch home a Hatfield?" shouted Sadie.

"Girl," Cal demanded, nudging my shoulder with the shotgun, "you got any Hatfield blood in them veins?"

"N-n-no, sir," I replied. "My name is Ginny Lucas. I'm not related to any Hatfields. In fact, I don't even know any Hatfields."

"What's your business out here?" Cal asked, with the gun still pointed toward me.

"I-I got lost from my cousins, Chelsea and Brad Brown." I added quickly, "They're not related to any Hatfields either. Sadie said you might know if they're in the area. If I could just find them, we'd be on our way, sir."

Cal rested the butt of his shotgun on the ground. He growled, "I'm a farmer, young'un. I been plowin' all day. How would I know about any fool cousins of yourn?"

Sadie interrupted, "Cal, quit actin' so uppity. I promised this young'un you'd hep her. You know dadburn well anytime a critter, be it two legged or four legged, sets foot in this here holler. Fess up, do you know anything 'bout her kin?"

To my surprise, Cal grinned and suggested, "No, I don't know nuthin' 'bout her kin. But if you and this here young'un go in and hep Ellie with the vittles, I'll mosey down to the Blue Goose Tavern and git the latest news."

"You ain't gonna mosey nowhere till you fetch me some water," called a shrill voice from the front porch.

Sadie waved as I stared in disbelief at Cal's wife, Ellie. She looked to be about my age, twelve, maybe thirteen. She was tiny with long, silken pale blonde curls falling to her waist. Her dress of cornflower blue matched her eyes. Her delicate features and dainty hands were like those of an angel. It was the corncob pipe she held between her teeth that shocked me. I had never seen any female smoke a pipe, let alone one my age.

"Woman, I wouldn't leave this yard without fetchin' your water," teased Cal as he reached for a wooden bucket hanging on the side of the barn.

While Cal was pumping the water, Sadie introduced me to her sister-in-law, Ellie. Ellie brought two cane-bottomed chairs out to the porch and asked us to sit a spell. She went back inside to get us cool drinks.

"Here, Sadie," whispered Cal, "give this to Ellie. I'd better git movin' lest she finds me more chores."

Cal sprinted to the barn and saddled up the white-spotted horse. He was galloping by the house when Ellie walked out on the porch with two tall glasses of milk.

"Cal, you'd better be back by supper!" she shouted. "And you'd better keep away from the Widow Sparks . . . and that white lightnin'. You hear me, Cal McCoy?"

Cal waved as he topped the hill. Ellie handed both Sadie and me a glass of milk. I eagerly took a big drink and began to choke. It was buttermilk, warm buttermilk. My hostess was smiling at me, waiting for a compliment; I was gagging, looking for a place to spit.

Sadie commented, "Ellie, you done a right nice job with this here buttermilk. You got it real smooth."

As Ellie turned to thank Sadie, I spit my mouthful of buttermilk into the yard. I poured out the rest of it through the wide cracks of the floor boards on the porch.

"She's right," I lied. "This is the best buttermilk I've ever tasted."

"There's more where that come from. Jest drink up," Ellie offered between puffs on the pipe. "I bet Cal ask you to hep me with the vittles? He don't think I cook so good, yet. But I'm a learnin'."

"Now, Ellie," Sadie said warmly, "if'n I'm gonna live here with you and my brother, I ought to hep with the chores."

"Where'd you come from, Ginny?" Ellie asked.

"I'm really from out west, California. I've been visiting my cousins from Welch, West Virginia," I replied.

"Californy! Californy! I ain't never seen nobody from out yonder.

Do all the womenfolk wear them men pants and black long johns like you a wearin'?''

I realized I was wearing my Grateful Dead T-shirt and Lee jeans. "Yes, but this is a T-shirt, not underwear. The Grateful Dead is a rock . . . I mean a music group."

Ellie moved closer to study my T-shirt. She remarked, "Me and Cal got our pitchers took when we got married. How do you reckon them guitar pickers and banjo pluckers got their pitchers on this here B-shirt?"

"T-shirt," I corrected. "*T* like in *table*. It's a T-shirt."

"I ain't much on spellin'," Ellie blushed, "but I did real good on cipherin'. Cal says I do numbers and make change real good."

I was embarrassed about my rude comment. "Oh, Ellie, I'm sure you're smart and good at lots of things. I think your dress and you . . . you're prettier than anyone I've ever seen in California," I exclaimed.

"Ah, you don't truly mean that, do you?" said Ellie blushing again.

I affirmed, "Yes, I do. You are really pretty."

"Tell me more about Californy. What kind of homeplace do you have? What does your husband do?" Ellie probed.

Sadie interrupted, "You young'uns can surely talk a blue streak. I'm a mite too old to care about Californy. I'm goin' catch forty winks, while you all talk about your menfolk." Sadie left her chair and shuffled into the house and disappeared.

Ellie flopped into Sadie's chair. "Tell me everything there is to know about Californy. Do you own any gold? What's it like way out yonder? Me and Cal probably never git out of Blackberry Holler."

I tried to answer Ellie's questions as best I could without having to explain about the one-hundred-year time difference. "California is not as green as Kentucky or West Virginia. I don't own any gold, nor does anyone else in my family. My dad works in an office . . . He's a book-keeper for a really large . . . general store. He hires people and tells them when to work. My mom is a dietician."

"I'm sorry 'bout your ma. Did she die birthin' a baby?" Ellie asked innocently.

"No," I explained gently. "She helps doctors and sick people with their meals."

"You mean a cook. I bet she's a blue ribbon winner," Sarah added.

I agreed and continued, "She is good at her job."

"You married yet?" Ellie questioned.

90

"Gosh, no," I answered. "I'm only twelve . . . almost thirteen. I go to Oakvale Middle School."

"Why, you poor thing," Ellie sympathized, "I guess that's why your ma and pa sent you back east. Menfolk must be scarce out west. Are you a fixin' to be a school marm?"

"Never would I want to be a teacher," I answered emphatically.

"Then why in blue blazes are you still goin' to school? You ain't one of them slow larnin' type, are you?" asked Ellie.

"The girls I know in California go to school a long time," I explained.

"With all that larnin' they're a gettin', I guess they don't have time to git a husband," Ellie concluded.

"How much learning do you have?" I opened my big mouth again. "I mean you seem really smart. I just wondered if you had to stay in school very long?"

"My ma and pa thought edication was 'portant. Me and my four sisters and six bruthers all 'tended school. We'uns went every year till we larned how to read and rite and cipher numbers." Ellie continued, "Now Cal, ain't got no school larnin', but I'm a teachin' him to rite his name and read the Good Book. Don't you dare breathe that to anuther soul, you hear."

Two shotgun blasts echoed in the distance. Ellie ran off the porch, shielded her eyes with her hand, and stood on tiptoe, as she tried to see where the shots came from. Sadie hurried onto the porch.

"Is it Cal?" Sadie asked.

"I don't think so," a frightened Ellie answered. "Cal don't usually signal with two shots. Besides, he ain't had time to get to town and back."

Two more shots, followed by wild yells, rang through the valley. Ellie darted toward the cow that was chewing grass near the rail fence. She slapped its hindquarters and guided it toward the barn. Sadie dashed back into the house and reappeared with a shotgun.

"Hurry, Ellie!" Sadie shouted to the young girl, as she closed the barn door and ran toward the house.

More shots and yells, this time much closer, sounded throughout the valley. Three riders appeared on top of the ridge just as Ellie reached the front porch.

"Young'uns, git inside," Sadie ordered with a voice of cold steel.

Ellie and I ran inside and closed the door. Sadie backed into the

91

shadows on the porch and brought the gun to her shoulder. The three riders stayed on top of the ridge, firing their guns in the air and shouting like wild Indians. They passed around a brown jug and each had a drink. One lone rider started down the hill toward the house. When his horse neared the far end of the fence, Sadie fired. The blast from the shotgun caused the windows to rattle and the horse to whinny. The rider reined in his horse while his noisy friends on top of the ridge stopped cold in their tracks.

"State your business, Floyd Hatfield," ordered Sadie, "while you are still able to talk."

"Good afternoon, Miss Sadie," Floyd replied, tipping his hat. "Me and my bruthers jest thought we'd pay a neighborly visit."

"You ain't never been neighborly and you ain't welcome here. Now you take those two varmints you call bruthers, and git out of here," ordered Sadie.

"Why, Miss Sadie," Floyd mocked, "don't you want to know why we cum to visit? We have some of your kinfolks back at Pappy's house."

Ellie slipped open the door and joined Sadie on the porch. She whimpered to Sadie, "They've got Cal. I know it; I just know it. What are we goin' . . . ?"

"Hush, woman, I'll handle this," snapped Sadie.

Sadie called to Floyd, "What's makes you think, 'course Hatfields is too dumb to think, that you fount you some McCoys?"

" 'Cause these critters we fount are too ugly and mean to be Hatfields," laughed Floyd. His brothers on the ridge whooped in agreement and fired their guns.

"What name do they go by?" questioned Sadie.

"They don't even lie good. They claim they're Browns, not McCoys." Floyd continued, "They got high fuluttin' society names, like Brad Lee and Sell Ces. Dress funny, too. Course if they ain't no kin of your'n, we'll jest throw 'em back into Tug River. That's where we fount 'em this mornin'."

I hurried onto the porch. I tried to push by Sadie to go and talk to the rider. She shoved me back, behind her.

"They're my cousins, Sadie," I whispered. "That's who I was telling you about this morning. Maybe he'll take me to them."

"Young'un," Sadie responded, "hush up. You can't trust no Hatfields. They is always up to no good."

Sadie stepped into the sunlight and lowered the gun to her waist.

92

"We ain't got no kin named Brown. We fount a young'un lost this mornin', too. She claims she's kin to them folks and they was a passin' through to West Virginny."

"Now is that a fact?" Floyd sneered. "Where is the young'un you fount?"

Sadie signaled for me to step into the light. I joined her and shouted, "She's right. They're my cousins. We're on our way to Welch. We don't want any trouble, sir. We'd just like to leave."

"You a McCoy and you don't want nary trouble?" laughed Floyd. "Now if that ain't funnier than Cal McCoy wallowin' in mud with a greased pig."

Ellie shouted, "You leave my man out of this, Floyd Hatfield! He can whoop you any day of the year!"

"Miss Ellie, don't you scare me so," mocked Floyd. "I'm jest shakin' like a leaf 'cause I'm afeared of Cal McCoy." In a cold, serious tone Floyd continued, "You give your man a message for me. Tell him his kin is locked up in my pappy's icehouse. They a gonna stay there till he makes a payment."

"A pay-ment?" gasped Sadie. "Jest what kind of a pay-ment are you a talkin' about?"

"Cal is kinda slow, but his missus is fairly smart. Maybe she can hep him think of somethin'." Floyd tipped his hat and rode up the hill toward his rowdy brothers. The three men shared drinks from the jug, shouted good-byes, fired several more shots, and then galloped over the ridge.

Sadie and Ellie just stared at me. I knew I was to blame for this ugly scene. I started to apologize, "I'm sorry. I didn't mean to cause any trouble between you and the Hatfields. I-I'll try and talk to them about this payment. I've got something they might want to trade for. Sadie, Ellie, would you take me to the Hatfield place?"

"Young'un, I promised to hep you and I will. But I can't rightly ask Ellie to get tangled up in this here mess," replied Sadie.

"I understand," I agreed. "All I want you to do is take me to the Hatfield place. Sadie, would you?"

"That's jest the same as askin' for her life," Ellie explained. "Do you know what Devil Anse would do to a McCoy if he caught 'em in West Virginny?"

"Then just tell me how to get there. You don't have to go with me. Would you, please, Sadie?" I begged.

"Young'un, how many times do I have to tell you? I aim to hep you," Sadie responded.

"Sadie," Ellie began, "you'd better not do nuthin' 'til Cal gets back. He don't want no kin of his'n goin' into Hatfield country . . . "

Sadie fired back, "Tarnation, girl, I'm sick and tired of Cal a tellin' me what I can and cannot do. Ain't no man livin' gonna tell me what to do."

Ellie hung her head, wiped her eyes, and started back inside the house.

"I guess I hert her feelins'," Sadie muttered.

"I'm sorry for all the trouble I've caused," I remarked.

"Ain't got time for sorries. Let's get a movin'," ordered Sadie.

"Can I run in and tell Ellie good-bye?" I asked.

"Young'un, we're only goin' be gone a couple of 'ours. You'll have all the time in the world to yak with Ellie once we git you and your kin back here," Sadie explained.

"I forgot about that," I lied.

Sadie shouldered her gun and motioned toward the ridge. "I got a short cut," she grinned, "we'll be at Devil Anse's place within an 'our."

We started up the hill and topped the ridge. Instead of heading back toward Blackberry Creek, we traveled at a fast pace along the top of the ridge for about a mile. I followed Sadie as she ducked under broken tree limbs, stepped wide around briar bushes, and steadied herself by holding onto wild grapevines. As we started down the far side of the ridge, Sadie raised her arm and signaled for us to sit and rest. We stretched out on the moss covered forest floor and gazed up at sparse patches of blue sky, filtering through the green leaf canopy of trees.

"Sadie," I asked, "why do you call this Mr. Hatfield Devil Anse?"

" 'Cause Anderson Hatfield is a devil," she retorted. "He's meaner than a rattlesnake and he fights like Lucifer himself. Durin' the Civil War he led a bunch of men from Logan County. They was Johnny Rebs and called theirselves Logan Wildcats. They was a fightin' some Northerners, back up yonder on the ridge. Ole Anse Hatfield got fired up and whooped the whole outfit of them northern boys single-handed. I hear'd tell he shot 'bout thirty of 'em and kilt the rest by cuttin' their throats. Ever since then, folks have called him Devil Anse."

"Is he still that mean?" I asked.

"Yep, fur as I know, he's still that mean," replied Sadie. "But you'll be findin' that out for yourself real soon. Look yonder, at the

94

bottom of the hill. See the smoke arisin' from that chimney twix them two persimmon trees? That there is Devil's house. We're here, young'un.''

I jumped to my feet and strained my eyes to see the house under the smoking chimney. "I can't see a house, let alone an icehouse."

"You got to follow this here path to the bottom of the hill. It'll brung you out pert near behind the icehouse. Now, young'un, listen good to me. I can't go down with you 'causin' them Hatfields might git lucky and grab me. I do all the doctoring for the McCoys . . . and Cal and Ellie need my hep a lot more'n I need theirn.''

"I know that, Sadie," I replied. "All I wanted you to do was bring me to the Hatfield place. I don't want anything to happen to you or any of your family.''

"Young'un," Sadie continued, "I do have somethin' that might hep you down thar with them varmits. Anse Hatfield gave me this here locket when I was . . . I guess about your age.''

Sadie pulled a tarnished oval silver locket out of her skirt pocket. She held it up to the light and studied the etched roses on the outer cover, as the long chain dangled from her hand. She opened the locket and looked hopelessly at the handsome man and young woman.

"That was many a summer ago," she whispered, as she held the locket to her heart.

"Did you know . . . did you date Devil Anse?" I asked.

"Date? I don't know about this here date business, Young'un, but I courted Anse for two years. I pert near wed the young fool," Sadie snapped, sounding like her old self again.

"Did you . . . did you love him?" I asked.

"Ain't no McCoy gonna hitch up with any Hatfield," assured Sadie.

"That's not what I asked," I said. "I asked if you loved him."

After a long pause Sadie replied in a forlorn voice, "It jest weren't in the stars. Our kin would never leave us be."

"I'm sorry. I really am, Sadie," I replied.

Sadie, with tears in her eyes, placed the locket in my palm and closed my fingers tightly around it. She patted my hand twice and turned around so that I couldn't see her loneliness and tears.

In a broken voice she ordered, "Now you fetch that locket with you, Ginny. If you git caught, make 'em take you to old Devil hisself. You jest show him that there locket. Tell him that's the payment."

"Oh, Sadie," I replied, "I can't take your locket. It means so much to you. I think you should keep it."

Sadie walked a few steps away from me. With her back to me she said, "I'm too old for that now." She continued as she turned around. "Young'un, are you waitin' for the whip-or-wills or are you goin' after your kin?"

I ran toward Sadie and embraced her. "Thank you, Sadie; thank you for everything."

"Now you hurry on," she said, as she pushed me away from her and toward the path. "I'll be waitin' for you and your folks on top of the ridge, next to them mossy rocks."

I put the locket in the pocket of my jeans and felt it scrape against the golden horseshoe. I never thought in a hundred years that I would have real gold and silver in my possession. I never thought I would be feuding with the Hatfields either. I waved at Sadie, as she started toward the top of the ridge.

I turned toward the Hatfield homestead with an uneasy feeling in my stomach. As I started downward, I stepped carefully along the path so as not to slip or make any noise. The roof of the icehouse, sitting over the creek, came into view. I hid behind a wide oak tree and studied the scene in front of me. The icehouse was about fifty yards from the main dwelling. It could be seen clearly from the side of the house, but not from the front porch. So I only needed to worry about someone spotting me from the two side windows. A huge barn towered behind the house, but the loft door was closed. The yard was vacant of all visible life, except for a hound dog that lay sleeping on the stone porch step in the warm afternoon sun. I searched the area again looking for Floyd, his brothers, or even Devil Anse. The emptiness and stillness of the scene made my hands sweat and my stomach quiver.

I was beginning to lose my courage. I told myself that I would run to the back of the icehouse on the count of five. One . . . two . . . three . . . four . . . GO! I jumped from behind the tree and ran as fast as I could toward the icehouse. Sharp stones and dry twigs jabbed my bare feet, but I was too frightened to look down at the crude ground. I kept my eyes glued to the icehouse. My feet splashed into icy cold water as I grabbed for the back corner of the rough wooden building. I fell back against the coarse timber and gasped for air. My heart pounded so desperately that my throat hurt. I tried calming down by telling myself I had two items to trade as ransom, the silver locket and the golden horseshoe. My mind panicked. What if Chelsea and Brad weren't in the icehouse? What if the Hatfield clan had killed them? What if this was . . .

"Ginny, Ginny, is that you?" a voice whispered.

"Chelsea," I cried, "oh, Chelsea, are you okay?"

"Just cold," Chelsea replied in her casual voice. "Where in the world have you been? We looked everywhere for you. How did you know where to find us?"

"Let's save twenty questions for later," interrupted Brad. "Ginny, I think the lock on the door is only a wooden pin through a metal ring. Can you find it and pull it out?"

I peeped around the side of the icehouse. "No problem," I answered as I could feel my fears leave and my confidence build.

"Be careful," warned Brad. "Mrs. Hatfield is at home and if she sees you . . . well, let's just say she is real handy with a gun."

I slipped around the corner and pulled the wooden pin out of the ring. The heavy door swung open with little effort. I stepped quickly inside and pulled the door shut.

"Straight ahead," Brad commanded, "your eyes will get use to the dim light."

As I moved toward the sound of his voice, my eyes began to focus on two seated figures tied with ropes. I knelt quickly next to Chelsea and started to loosen her bonds. When she twisted her arms free, she gave me a warm hug.

"Remember me? I'm the frozen cousin sitting on a block of ice with my hands and feet still tied?" taunted Brad.

"Help Brad," Chelsea said. "I can untie my own feet. What happened to you, Gin? We looked everywhere for you."

As I untied Brad, I explained to Chelsea, "It's a long story. I ran into a mountain woman by the name of Sadie McCoy. She helped me . . . "

"I've had enough of mountain men and mountain women," Brad declared. "Do you have the horseshoe?"

I responded, "Yes, of course. It's in my pocket."

"Then let's get out of this place and travel," Brad said as he took Chelsea and me by the hand and led us toward the door.

He opened the door slightly and surveyed the yard and house through the narrow slit. He turned toward us in the dim light.

"Just open the door enough to slip out and run around to the back. Try not to make any noise splashing in the water. Once we get on the back side, we'll head for the river. It's not that deep so we can wade across. We'll be on the Kentucky side then. Any questions?'' he whispered.

"But Sadie is waiting for us on top of the ridge," I said. "She'll help us get back home, or at least to safety."

"Ginny," Brad ordered, "we've got to get out of here now. It's too dangerous. I don't know who this Sadie is, or if she can be trusted. I think it's best to . . . "

Shots rang out from the top of the ridge. The sound of angry men shouting and galloping horses crashing though underbrush rolled down the mountain as the riders headed toward the house.

"Do you think they've found Sadie?" I cried. "She was only trying to help me."

"Hurry," said Brad as he pulled Chelsea and me through the door.

"Brad, I've got to go back and see if Sadie is okay!" I cried.

Brad grabbed my arm and pulled me back against the icehouse. He squeezed my wrist with anger. "Ginny, you head for that hill and we'll all be killed," he said.

"But she's waiting . . . " I began.

Brad jerked my arm as Chelsea watched in disbelief. He explained, "The Hatfields think we're still in the icehouse. If they see you running toward the hill, they'll know you've tried to help us. We'll end up dead meat."

"He's right, Ginny," Chelsea said, "we can't risk you begin caught."

Whoops and laughter floating from the homestead were shattered by a woman's piercing scream. After a few second of silence a somber voice boomed, "Let her be."

"But Sadie was on that ridge because she trusted and helped me. If it wasn't for her, I wouldn't be here and you wouldn't be out of that icehouse," I said. "I can't just leave her now, not when she is in trouble."

I pulled my arm away and rubbed my sore wrist. I reached into my pocket and pulled out the locket and the horseshoe. I handed the horseshoe to Brad.

"Here, you take it. I'm going to try and help Sadie."

"Ginny, don't, it won't work," Chelsea pleaded.

"I won't let you do that," Brad said, grabbing me from behind and putting one hand over my mouth. He carried me about fifteen feet away from the icehouse and stumbled behind a wood pile. Chelsea followed at his heels. From behind the stacked wood I could see Sadie standing boldly in the midst of four men. A lanky bearded man, dressed in black, stepped off the porch and extended his hand to Sadie.

"I don't reckon you heard me right," he said. "I said to let her be."

Brad reached for the horseshoe in my hand. I gave it up willingly, since I had secretly decided to stay and help Sadie if it was necessary. He turned the golden horseshoe over and over in his hand, trying to pick up a beam of light. I tried to scoot away from him, but each time I moved he slid next to me. Chelsea sensed what was happening and moved in against me from the other side. As I sat wedged between my cousins, I thought of the locket. I pulled it out of my pocket and struggled to stand up.

"Brad," I pleaded, "just let me return this locket to Sadie. She and Devil Anse used to be an item. If he knew that she had kept this locket after all these years, I bet . . . "

The blinding light that suddenly bolted from the locket to the horseshoe was jagged, like lightning. It flashed again. The locket glowed red and then amber as the horseshoe began to rise from Brad's hand and spin. I held the locket tightly.

"No," I cried to an unknown power, "this is Sadie's. It belongs to her."

I tried to dart from behind the pile of wood toward Sadie and the men, but Brad tackled me. I clutched the locket in my left hand as I reached for the rising horseshoe.

"Stop it," I pleaded. "I can't go yet, not until Sadie is all right."

I watched in despair as the horseshoe continued to rise and spin. Light flashed repeatedly from the locket to the horseshoe. I pulled the locket under my body hoping to block the light and halt the time travel. I realized it wasn't working as the ground around me continued to spin and the bright light blinded me. I felt paralyzed; Brad held on to my legs and Chelsea brushed against my arm. Mentally I yielded to the spinning, flashing horseshoe that signaled another journey.

Facts

1. The cures and signs related by the fictitious Sadie McCoy were Appalachian remedies used by pioneers and Indians in early western Virginia.

99

2. Devil Anse (Anderson Hatfield) received his nickname by single-handedly killing a band of Union soldiers. He did command a Confederate regiment from Logan County known as the *Logan Wildcats*.

3. Reasons for the Hatfield-McCoy feud vary among historians. Some feel it grew out of the Civil War. The Hatfields were Confederate and the McCoys were Union. Others trace its origin to the election-day killing of Ellison Hatfield (brother of Devil Anse) by the three sons of Randolph McCoy. Some historians actually believe the feud was caused when Floyd Hatfield stole a pig from Ranel McCoy. Romantics like to believe the feud was a result of an ill-fated romance between Johnse Hatfield (the fun loving son of Devil Anse) and Roseanna McCoy (the daughter of the McCoy clan leader, Randolph McCoy).

4. The Hatfields, led by Anderson (Devil Anse) Hatfield, lived in Logan County, West Virginia. The McCoys, united under Randolph McCoy, lived across the Tug River in Pike County, Kentucky.

5. The feud began in 1882 and was responsible for approximately twenty deaths. It gained national attention when Governor Buckner of Kentucky sent officials to arrest some Hatfields in West Virginia. Governor Wilson of West Virginia sued for their release, but the United States Supreme Court upheld the state of Kentucky in the matter of extradition (the turning over of an alleged criminal from one state to another).

Sinkhole where sheep-killing dogs were thrown. This is where three of the McCoys were tied to pawpaw trees along Blackberry Creek and shot by members of the Hatfield family.

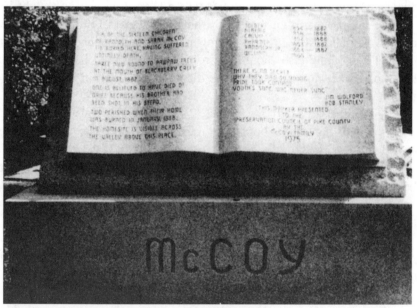

McCoy monument erected on the original homesite in 1975 to mark six of the sixteen graves of family members who died during the feud.

Chapter 7

Mine Wars

Red, gold, and then blinding white, the light was incredible. Tears trickled down my face from my burning eyes. I didn't want to open them. I had the strange feeling the if I opened my eyes I wouldn't be home. The breath-taking spinning had stopped, but my stomach was still queasy. My left hand ached and burned. I wished I had never come to West Virginia.

"Ginny, Ginny," Brad said softly, "you can get up now. I'm sorry about tackling you, but we couldn't take a chance on getting caught."

I felt Brad's arm loosen from around my legs as I blinked my eyes opened. I pulled myself to a sitting position and opened my hand. I thought something else should be in my hand with the horseshoe. The lone horseshoe, now with only one diamond, sparkled in the afternoon sun.

Ignoring Brad's apology, I said, "I had something else in my hand other than this horseshoe, but I can't remember what it was. Do you have any idea what I had?"

"I just remember being cold, really cold. I'm glad it's warmer here," Chelsea responded while she rubbed her arms.

"I know I had something else in my hand," I insisted, "and it was important to me. There was someone else . . . I needed to help."

"Gin," Brad began, "I remember you trying to leave. It was important we stay together, so I tackled you. But for the life of me, I can't remember why or if you had anything else in your hand."

I sat confused and puzzled, trying to remember what had just happened. I kept hearing thundering horses and a piercing scream, probably that of a bobcat, in the back of my mind. I must have run from a bobcat, and Brad tackled me to save me. I guess we traveled instead of facing the mountain lion. The sound of Chelsea's voice brought me to the present.

"Black water! I swear I saw black water. It feels like water and it runs in a creek like water, but it's black," babbled Chelsea.

"Sure, and the mountains are candy and the sky is buttermilk," Brad chuckled.

"Don't you laugh at me, Brad Brown," snapped Chelsea. "If you're so smart, Mr. Know-it-all, why don't you get us home?"

After noticing the normal looking green trees, blue sky, white clouds, and dirt road, I asked, "Where did you see black water? This place looks pretty normal to me. We're just out in the woods again."

"Okay, you unbelievers, just follow me," insisted Chelsea as she signaled us to follow.

We left the grassy area and walked toward a small clump of trees. The sound of water mingled with a peculiar odor as we passed through the trees. Chelsea was right. I couldn't believe my eyes! The water running in the little creek was jet black. The bank looked normal as it sloped downward, but all rocks and soil disappeared under the foreboding black liquid.

"It feels like water," Brad remarked, swishing his hand in the ebony substance.

Chelsea warned, "I wouldn't do that if I were you. You might not have a hand after all that pollution."

"Speaking of pollution, take a look at that mountain," I suggested. "It's all black pieces of rock and it's smoldering. Maybe that's what we're smelling. Phew."

"It looks like we just missed a huge forest fire. Look at all those dead trees on either side of that mountain," exclaimed Chelsea.

"A forest fire wouldn't cause a creek to run black water," Brad remarked. "Besides, what we're smelling is more like rotten eggs than burned timber."

"Pardon me, brother genius, for even guessing," sneered Chelsea. "Besides, what we're smelling is you."

"Oh, you two, knock it off. You make me homesick for David. Believe me, that is really sick," I said.

Chelsea blurted, "Now where in the world are we?"

"Beats me. This is your state, remember," I answered.

"The future," Brad replied. "That's it! We're in the future! Pollution has caused the water to turn black and our mountains to burn. I've figured out the diamonds and sapphires, too."

"This should be good, really good," commented Chelsea as she rolled her eyes.

"Don't you see? This is the purpose of these trips," Brad insisted.

"I'm sorry, Brad. I don't follow you," I responded.

"Now listen up, you two." Brad spoke with authority. "These trips are just to let us know what our state was like and what it will be like, if we don't clean up our streams, stop the strip mining and put some air quality controls on the chemical plants in the Kanawha Valley."

"Boy genius," interrupted Chelsea, "we hear that constantly in school, over the radio, on TV, and from the legislature. Why a time trip? Why us? And don't leave out the part about the diamonds and sapphires."

Brad angrily answered, "I don't have all the answers. I'm not sure, why us. But I have figured out the missing diamonds and sapphires. Every place we have visited, we have left something behind, but we have gained some knowledge about our state."

"Yeah, we have really gained a lot of knowledge. Ginny can't even remember what she had in her hand, and none of us know what happened to our tennis shoes," said Chelsea, as she folded her arms and rolled her eyes a second time.

"Forget it. Just forget it. There is no use wasting my breath to try and explain anything to a female as mule-headed as you," said Brad.

"Shhh, I hear something," I warned.

Two boys about twelve years old appeared from the clump of trees. They wore baggy long jeans, plain white T-shirts, and black tennis shoes. The tall, thin blonde boy had a wooden baseball bat with an old fashioned pitcher's glove hung over the knob across his right shoulder. The shorter, dark-haired boy was tossing a homemade baseball up in the air. Both boys froze in their tracks when they saw us.

"Hey, how're you doing, guys?" said Brad, trying to break the uncomfortable silence. "Going to play some ball?"

"Yeah," replied the blonde boy, "we thought we'd hit a few."

"Need a few more players?" Brad offered.

The two boys looked at each other and smiled. "We don't play with girls," the dark-haired boy replied.

"I don't either," Brad quickly put in, "but my folks are . . . real busy and I promised to keep an eye on the girls."

"Where're you from?" the blonde boy asked. "I've never seen you in camp before."

"Uh, w-we just moved into camp," I said.

"Did you move into the Hicks's place?" the blonde boy asked.

"Nah," Brad replied, "but we're real close to it."

"Gee." The dark-haired boy's eyes widened. "You must be the new super's kids."

"That's right," Chelsea blurted out. "I'm Chelsea, that's my brother Brad, and this is our cousin, Ginny. And who might you two be?"

The blonde-haired boy moved toward us, smiling as he said, "I'm Ronnie and this is my best friend, Tony. I guess our dads will be working for your dad in the mines. We were just going over to the slate dump to hit a few balls."

"We've got to get ready for this big game against Cabin Creek," Tony added. "If we win this one, the company will buy us all new uniforms. Last year we almost . . . "

Chelsea interrupted, "Last year . . . now that would have been. Mmm, what year was that Tony?"

A puzzled Tony answered, "Last year was 1920. We almost beat Cabin Creek. This year we will for sure. Ronnie is the fastest pitcher around. He can hit, run and do just about everything."

Ronnie blushed and kicked at the dirt. Chelsea shot a quick glance toward Brad and mouthed 1920.

"We can always use an extra player," Ronnie said, looking at Brad. "We just lot Buddy Hicks when his dad got . . . got k-killed in the slate fall. But I guess you know about that."

"But we can't have girls on the team," Tony added, looking apologetically at Chelsea and me. "That's like having a woman in a coal mine. Everybody knows, that's bad luck."

"We know that," I added before Chelsea could explode on them. "Is it okay if we just watch you guys practice up at the dump?"

The boys studied each other for a few seconds and then Ronnie answered, "I guess it's okay. We don't want any trouble with the super."

"I think I'd go home and get some shoes first," Tony suggested, staring at our bare feet. "The old super had a work crew pack red dog and throw a little dirt on the field, but you still can't go barefoot up there."

"We didn't think about that," commented Chelsea. "We're used to grass not red . . . red cat. I mean red dog."

"Did you live in Charleston?" Ronnie asked.

"Yes," lied Chelsea. "This is the first time Dad has brought us to a camp. Maybe you guys can give us some pointers on how to live out here."

Ronnie glanced in Tony's direction and then said, "What do you mean, 'to live out here'?"

I butted in, "She means things like we should wear our shoes all the time. In Charleston we didn't play on a slate dump."

"I guess you had a lot of level ground," said Tony. "Down here we live in this narrow hollow. The company dumps slate in the back of the hollow. After a while it gets high enough to level out with the mountains on either side. Mr. Blevins sent a crew up to level it out and throw some red dog and dirt on it. Red dog is nothing but clinkers."

"Clinkers, what are clinkers?" asked Chelsea.

"You've got to excuse my sister. She has never been out of Charleston before. She's a real city slicker," commented Brad.

"You take clinkers out of your stove after you burn coal," Ronnie said. "They're like big chunks of rock about the size of your fist and they're red. You can run fast over them, but you sure don't want to slide. Mr. Blevins had the men put dirt on the infield and pack it down. It has to be a close game before you slide there, too."

"What about the smoke and that sulfur odor from the smoldering slate? Isn't that stuff dangerous?" asked Brad.

"It's smokes all the time," Tony answered, "and you get used to the smell. It's no worse than the outhouses during the summer."

Ronnie added, "It's not dangerous unless you fall asleep up there for a long time. I heard my mom and dad talking about some wino that would sleep near the dump during the winter to keep warm. One night he must've breathed in too many fumes, they found him dead the next day."

"Do your parents know that you go up there to play?" asked Chelsea.

"Sure," Tony responded. "We're either here or at the swimming hole every day."

"We have to go outside to play or even talk to each other. Both our dads work 'hoot-owl,' so they sleep during the day," Ronnie explained.

"*Hoot-owl* means 'midnight shift,' " remarked Brad with a know-it-all look.

"It's no fun being quiet all day," said Tony.

106

"What about your brothers and sisters?" I asked. "What do they do all day?"

"I only have one older brother, Ray," Ronnie explained proudly. "He's fifteen and gets to work in the mines with Dad. He got a real silver dollar from the section boss because he loaded more coal than any grown man on the shift last week."

Chelsea mumbled, "Future. My brilliant brother thought we were in the future."

"He's the lucky one; he has a brother. I have six sisters," Tony said with a wide grin. "Mama puts them all to work. They have to help with the garden, house, laundry, and the twins. Theo has a job at the company store, but she still helps Mama with supper. I help my dad with the man's work. We make the wine. It's pretty good, too. You'll find out because Dad always gives a bottle to the super at Christmas."

"Tell me about your school," I said.

Ronnie shrugged and said, "A school is a school. My school probably isn't as big or fancy as your Charleston school, but it'll do."

"How many rooms? How many students?" I probed.

"Just one room. All our schoolhouses are just one room. The company built it and they give the teacher a house to live in. It goes to the eighth grade, but only girls stay in school that long. Most of the guys start to work in the mines when they're needed," Tony announced.

"Or if their parents will let them," Ronnie added.

"Ronnie is still going to school with a bunch of girls," offered Tony. "His mama thinks he's too smart to quit. She doesn't like the idea of his brother working in the mines, either. She thinks Ray's smart, too."

Chelsea began, "Then why did she . . . "

After seeing Ronnie redden, Brad interrupted, "I think we ought to head back to camp with you guys. I'm afraid we've wasted your baseball playing afternoon. Those look like storm clouds ahead."

We turned and surveyed the dark sky. Then we started into the clump of trees through the clearing and toward the camp.

Chelsea stopped us all when she shouted, "Wait a minute. Ronnie, Tony, do you know there is a creek back there full of black water?"

Both boys looked at each other, nodded, and smiled.

"Sure," said Ronnie. "Do you think we're stupid? Everybody knows where Campbell Creek is."

"But does everybody know that it runs *black*?" Chelsea proclaimed.

A puzzled Tony asked, "What color do you expect it to be?"

107

"Clear, clean. You ought to be able to see the bottom," exclaimed Chelsea.

"Are the creeks and rivers in Charleston clear? Can you see the bottoms?" Ronnie asked.

"Of course you can."

"Maybe they just don't mine as much coal as we do," replied Ronnie with a shrug.

"What does mining coal have to do with the creek running black?" I asked.

Ronnie looked at Brad and realized all three of us were puzzled. He replied, "The company washes the coal in a sluice to get any blasting powder or dust off it. The creek is channeled through the sluice and over the coal. The clean coal is then loaded into railroad cars at the tipple. The creek is channeled back to its original bed. It's really pretty neat to watch."

Chelsea jabbed Brad with her elbow and mumbled, "We've been sent to the future to warn people about pollution . . . "

"Shut up or you'll blow our cover," Brad muttered under his breath.

"Where do you get your water to drink?" I asked.

"A well," Tony added. "Everyone has a well. We're lucky that our dads work for Coppercoal . . . "

Chelsea interrupted, "Do tell me why you are so lucky."

Tony, unaware of Chelsea's tone, continued, "All the kitchens in the camp, every house, has a pump in the kitchen sink. Our mamas don't have to carry in water with buckets."

Chelsea whispered under her breath, "I don't think I can handle this great future."

"Since we all know why the creek is black, don't you think we should get back to the coal camp? That sky is really getting dark," Brad suggested.

The group of five fell into step with Ronnie and Brad in the lead. Tony placed himself between Chelsea and me and offered his hand any time we needed assistance. The narrow dirt road dropped sharply around each bend until it leveled off at the railroad crossing. Once the band crossed the tracks the coal camp came into view. A neat whitewashed row of one story frame houses, protected by white picket fences, sat on the left side of the tracks. Patches of green grass behind the fences contrasted with the bare ground, blackened by coal dust, separating the yards from the tracks. On the right side of the tracks, perched on the side of the mountain, was a similar row of eight houses. These small homes lacked the grassy yards, and their white exteriors had been dimmed by the puffing smoke of coal trains. Small children played on front porches or in grassy yards, as the women hurriedly took the wash off the clothes lines. Older children, in groups of threes and fours, were skipping or running up the dirt street and into the houses to beat the approaching storm.

"We're at the far end," Ronnie said as he quickened his pace. "I'm sure my mom won't mind if you stay at my house until the storm is over."

"Gee, thanks," Brad said. "We'd sure appreciate it."

"Or you could stay with me," Tony offered. "Mama wouldn't notice three more people."

Thunder clapped and lightning flashed across the sky. We followed Ronnie as he began to run toward a large two-story building that earlier had been hidden from view by a huge beech tree. We dashed up the four wide steps and through the front door just as large raindrops pelted our heads and arms. We stumbled over one another trying to get inside.

"Don't drip on that material," a woman's voice snapped.

All five of us jumped back from the colorful bolts of cotton standing upright on the counter in front of the door. We backed against a table loaded with men's drab green work clothes. A pinched face woman with a shrill mean voice rushed at us.

"Look at you. Dirty as pigs," she scolded.

I looked down at my feet to escape her gaze. She was right. My feet were as black as the coal dust I had just run through, except for a gray splash caused by a stray raindrop or two. Even my arms and clothes seemed to have a fine layer of black soot on them.

"We're not going to touch anything," Ronnie promised. "As soon as the worst of the storm is over, we're going to my house."

"Go on now," she demanded. "I'll have to mop this floor again, because you were up to no good. If you kids would stay at home instead of . . ."

"Lillian, just leave them be," said a middle-aged mustached man counting coins from behind the cash register. "You kids just try and stay in one spot. When the storm lets up I'll have to ask you to leave."

"Uhm," Lillian grunted as she stomped away and disappeared behind a rack of women's dresses.

"Is this a J-Mart?" asked Chelsea, gazing around the store.

"It seems to have everything," I replied as I surveyed its products. One section looked like a grocery store with canned food stacked in pyramid shapes behind a butcher's meat counter. Another area had clothes for men, women, and children piled on tables or hung on racks. A third division had small appliances, tools, two scooters, a long sled, and one bicycle. The last unit had seeds, bags of rock salt, lanterns, blankets, a few lamps, and metal bunk bed frames. The floor that Lillian was going to mop was as black as the coal dust and felt sticky with oil. I didn't know if the odor that tickled my nose came from the oily floor or the gas lamps that burned dimly on the second floor balcony.

"Are there people up there?" I asked, looking toward the open balcony on the second floor.

"Yes," Tony answered quickly. "My sister Theo works up there. She is a bookkeeper," he announced proudly.

"This is the company store," Ronnie said. "Did you see the bicycle, the red one?"

"That sure looks like a big, heavy bike," Brad commented.

"My brother and I have one just like that," Ronnie stated proudly. "They only get one a year. My mom and dad saved enough scrip to get us one for Christmas last year. We're not allowed to let just anyone ride, but I'm sure Dad will . . ."

Chelsea interrupted, "They saved what?"

"Scrip," Ronnie said. "They saved enough scrip to buy us a bicycle for Christmas. They do have bicycles in Charleston, don't they?"

"Yeah, we have bicycles all right," said Chelsea. "But what is scrip? A coupon or box top?"

Ronnie chuckled, "It's just scrip. It's what you use when you buy something. It's money."

"But not real money," Brad explained.

Tony interjected, "It is so real. You can buy anything with it."

"But only here, at the company store," Brad insisted.

Ronnie, a little unsure and unwilling to admit Brad was completely right, ordered, "Tony, see if Theo will loan you some scrip?"

Tony, without saying a word, glanced over his shoulder to see if the storekeeper and his pinched-face wife were watching. Noting that they were occupied, he darted toward the back of the store, slipping between rows of boots and dinner pails. He paused at the bottom of a narrow staircase and then disappeared in the shadows.

"Will he get in trouble for going up there?" I questioned Ronnie.

110

"Nah," he replied, "Mrs. Bruce fusses a lot but she really likes kids."

"How can you tell?" Chelsea asked.

"You don't know her like we do," Ronnie explained. "We stop by nearly every day, and she always gives us ice cream on a stick. She just fusses about things getting dirty to remind the store clerk how hard she works."

A train whistle sounded in the distance, and the frame building began to vibrate. Bells clanged, and the engine rumbled as the building began to shake. The store clerk seemed to ignore the deafening noise as he continued to count the coins.

I grabbed Chelsea with one hand and the counter with the other. "Is that an earthquake or a train?" I asked, as the lanterns hanging overhead swayed back and forth.

"It's the Powhatan Arrow," Ronnie answered. "It comes through twice a day. It must be five-thirty. It's never late."

As the train lumbered by large glass windows of the store front, black smoke poured from the engine, and sparks flashed from the metal wheels screeching on the track. Cinders and fine dust sprayed from under the cars, as six passenger coaches and twenty-two coal cars rumbled by. A red caboose signaled the end of the train, for the rumble and roar of the engine softened and the building began to steady. The smoke, cinders, and dust hung in the air for a few seconds and then covered the complete area with a fine, oily black dust. Even the raindrops seemed black as they splashed against the window glass.

"It felt like an earthquake!" I exclaimed. "How do you stand that twice a day?"

Ronnie said, "We have trains go through here all the time. You just get use to it. Shucks, our house shakes more than this store. Mom tried once to put pictures on the wall but they kept falling off."

"Do they come through at night, too?" Chelsea asked.

"I guess. Yes," Ronnie replied, "they do run at night. I guess I just sleep through it. But without the . . ."

Tony appeared from behind the fabric counter with a frightened look on his face. "We got to get out of here. Theo said we are to go now, even if it's raining."

"Why? What happened?" Ronnie demanded.

"I can't say," Tony said, as he glanced over his shoulder. "Not here, anyway. Come on, Ronnie, we've got to go."

"Let's go; follow me." Ronnie turned toward the door.

We followed Ronnie and Tony into the rain that had slackened to a drizzle. We bounded down the steps and turned sharply to the left. We passed six more small, white square houses with smoky gray windows, a vacant lot covered with weeds, and a frame church with a bell tower. We crossed to the right side of the road in front of the church and ducked inside a vacant tool shed.

"Did anything happen at the mines?" Ronnie asked in a flat voice.

"Not yet," Tony blurted out. "Theo said a trainload of striking miners came through on the twelve o'clock train. They had thrown the company men off and were taking the train to Logan. They had guns, lots of ammunition, and even nurses. Theo said to go home and tell our parents."

"The union. Dad said the union would cause a war," Ronnie muttered.

"What will your papa do?" Tony asked Ronnie.

"He'll fight. After they sealed the mines to stop the fire, you remember, with Mr. Hicks still inside, Dad was really mad. He said the company just wanted to sell coal; they didn't care how many miners died."

I felt like an intruder, listening to the boys share their private thoughts. I suggested, "Maybe you should go home like Tony's sister told you to do."

"Yeah," Brad agreed. "This sounds real important. You'd better let your parents know."

Ronnie asked Tony, "What about your dad?"

Tony replied, "You know if your dad goes, my papa will go and take the rest of the Italians. Theo said the company will throw us out of our houses. You don't think they will, do you Ronnie?"

"They threw the miners out at Camp Creek. I guess they'll throw us out, too," Ronnie answered.

"Wait a minute," Chelsea remarked. "Nobody can throw you out of your home."

"It's not our home," Ronnie explained. "The company owns all these houses. If you lose your job—and believe me if you go on strike, you will lose your job—you have to get off their property. That means you must leave. I guess we could go stay with Aunt Blanche?"

"Don't you have any money saved?" Brad asked.

"Scrip, but only Coppercoal Stores will take our scrip," Ronnie replied.

"I forgot," said Tony digging into his pocket. "Here, Theo give us seventy-five cents."

He held out his hand with five coins; two about the size of quarters, two shaped like dimes and one a little larger than a nickel. All the coins had a small C cut out of the center and the name Coppercoal stamped around the edge. He dropped the light weight coins into my hand. They had a tinny sound.

"You mean they don't pay people real money? Just this funny money?" Chelsea exclaimed.

"That's all any coal company uses," Ronnie responded.

"Ronnie, I've got to get home. Theo made me promise I'd help Mama get ready to move," explained Tony.

"I'd better do the same," Ronnie commented. "Mom will really be upset when she hears the miners are carrying guns."

"You guys go ahead," Brad suggested. "We'll go down to the main offices and wait for our parents. I hope everything turns out all right."

Brad extended his hand to Ronnie for a handshake. The younger boy looked at him and stepped backward. "Your dad is a superintendent, a company man. I guess he'll be on the other side?"

Tony stared at us as if we had turned green before his eyes. He nodded at Ronnie and both boys left the shed without uttering another word.

"Why do I feel so rotten?" asked Chelsea. "I haven't done anything wrong."

"I have the same feeling," I said. "Brad, what do you know about this union and why would they want to fight?"

"This is a stormy part of our state's history," Brad began. "Most of the mines are owned by out-of-state businessmen. Some of these big shots have never been to West Virginia and have no idea how the common miner lives. They hire superintendents to run their mines. These supers aren't all bad, but they catch it from both sides. The owners are only interested in making money. If the super doesn't make money for them, he's fired. In order to make lots of money the company cuts benefits from their miners."

"You're losing me, big brother," remarked Chelsea. "Just get to the point."

"The miners are treated like dirt. They work ten to twelve hours a day in terrible conditions. Some miners must dig coal lying on their bellies or standing in water. Others are forced to go down into mines which are known to have gas, and that's deadly," explained Brad.

"Why don't they notify the Department of Interior?" I asked.

"It hasn't been formed yet," Brad replied. "At this time in history, if a miner complains, he is fired. If he is fired, he must move immediately out of the company house and he is blackballed."

Chelsea interrupted, "Blackballed?"

"His name is put on a list as a troublemaker. This list is passed around to other mine owners, and nobody will hire him," Brad stated.

"Then why don't they just leave the state?" I asked.

"How? Most of these miners are immigrants from Italy, Hungary, and Poland," Brad continued. A lot of them don't speak English. They came to West Virginia because they mined coal in Europe. This was a job they could do in America. Coal companies offered them a house to live in, food and supplies on credit, and free medical care. The immigrants poured into the state."

"If they're working they could save their money and leave," Chelsea suggested.

"Money was another thing," said Brad. "Miners were paid with scrip. This was money coined by the coal company; it's not legal tender."

"Keep it simple," warned Chelsea.

"I'm sorry. I forgot to whom I was speaking," sneered Brad. "Legal tender is money coined or printed by the U.S. government. It's like our money today, you can spend it anywhere in the United States. Scrip can only be spent in a store owned by the coal company that coined it."

"That's a real bummer," I concluded. "You work in horrid conditions, and if you complain you lose your job and get kicked out of your house. You're not even paid with real money, so how could you go anywhere else or even feed your family?"

"Exactly," Brad replied.

"You still haven't explained about the union," Chelsea reminded Brad.

"It's an organization of miners, a huge organization. Its purpose is to protect a miner's rights. A miner has the right to an eight-hour workday, safe working conditions, and real money. In a union the workers unite; they stick together. For example, if you refuse to go into a mine that you know is filled with gas, the company can't fire you or replace you."

114

"Replace you," I remarked. "Who would replace you? Who would be crazy enough to go into a mine that has gas?"

"A scab," Brad answered.

"Yuk!" Chelsea exclaimed.

"That's the name you call a worker who comes in and takes your job. If you had a family, and they were starving, you would be willing to take another man's job if he refused to work," explained Brad. "Union members won't do that to each other. They believe if one worker refuses to work, all workers should refuse to work until the violation is corrected."

Chelsea remarked, "Good for them."

"Not always," said Brad. "Sometimes they end up in jail."

"That's not fair," I said.

"It is if that's the law," Brad remarked. "Most mine owners . . . "

"Shh," whispered Chelsea. "Do you hear that noise? It sounds like men marching."

I moved to the door of the tool shed and peeped through a wide crack. I gasped at the sight of more than two hundred men marching like an army down the narrow road. Some were dressed in bib overalls, while others wore work clothes like the ones I saw in the company store. Several men wore pork pie hats, and a few others wore caps. All the men carried weapons and had red bandannas tied around their necks. One man walked alongside the group and gave orders like an army sergeant. At the end of the marchers was a wagon loaded with wooden crates covered by canvas. Two women, dressed in white nurse's uniforms complete with caps, sat up front with the driver. The men shouted for the villagers to join them and head for Blair Mountain. The men started to chant something about Sid Hatfield died so the heavens will weep. I couldn't understand all the words. I rushed to another crack on the far side of the shed to see the rest of the procession. On the front porch of one of the houses I could see a man kissing his wife goodbye. He left the porch and turned to wave to his family. It was . . .

"Ronnie's dad is joining the marchers!" I shouted.

Chelsea and Brad rushed to my side of the shed. Chelsea pushed me gently aside to peer out.

"I see him," she remarked. "Poor Ronnie, I think he's crying. There is a dark-complected man joining him. Do you think it's Tony's papa?"

Several voices crying and a woman's wail drifted into the moist air.

115

I found another crack to see through. Ronnie started to leave the porch, but his mother grabbed his arm. A taller boy, probably Ronnie's brother, ran off the porch with a rifle. He gave the rifle to his dad and then returned to the house.

I moved back toward the door and tried to spy the source of crying. It was Tony's sisters. They huddled around a large woman in the center of the yard, as she wept loudly and called her good-byes in Italian. Tony's dad moved into the middle of the last row of men. He was joined by other new recruits from the camp. The wagon with the nurses passed slowly in front of the tool shed, cutting off my view of the marchers.

"Where are they going?" I asked.

"I don't know, but let's follow," suggested Brad.

"Do you really think we should?"

"Why not? If it gets dangerous we'll just travel," Chelsea offered.

Brad asked, "You do have the horseshoe, don't you?"

I pulled the golden horseshoe out of my pocket for my cousins to see. "Of course. What if they won't let us follow them? What if . . . "

"I've got an idea," Brad said. "Just go along with it. When the people in the camp go inside, we'll try to catch that wagon."

"Do you expect me to run without shoes on that awful road just to catch up with a wagon?" Chelsea asked.

Brad said, "No, stupid, I expect you to fly."

"The people are going inside now," I said.

"Good," Brad said. "Now look, girls, that wagon isn't too far ahead of us. Once we catch the wagon, I'll try to hitch us a free ride."

"Where are we going?"

Brad replied, "We're going as far as they'll let us. Ready? Let's go."

We darted out of the shed and ran single file through the thin layer of wet black mud that covered the road. We left the rows of square houses with picket fences as soon as we rounded the bend. The road ahead was tree-lined and full of gray, dusky shadows. No houses or marchers were in sight. We ran silently for several minutes, trying to see or hear the marchers ahead.

Chelsea, panting and sweating, asked, "How do you know we're on the right road?"

"Chelsea, this is the only road; there are no turns. They've got to be up ahead."

116

"Shh." Brad signaled with his hand for us to stop. He motioned for us to leave the road and hide in a clump of bushes.

The sound of a horse and buggy racing at top speed filled the air. The crack of a whip signaled the appearance of a huge black horse snorting and galloping. The driver in the buggy stood with the reins in one hand and a whip in the other. The whip lashed the back of the horse, as the buggy made the turn on two wheels. Man, buggy, and horse drove past us and toward the marchers up ahead.

"We should have asked for a ride," teased Chelsea.

Brad rolled his eyes and signaled for us to get back on the road. We had gone only a few feet when we heard a commotion ahead—angry shouting, cursing, horses neighing, wagon brakes screeching, and guns firing echoed in the narrow hollow.

"Hurry," ordered Brad. "They're not too far ahead. This is the time to catch them."

We followed Brad when he sprinted down the road. The trees blurred as I ran as hard as I could to keep up with my cousins. I was relieved to see Brad signal for us to stop and leave the road. We moved about ten feet into the woods and hid behind some rhododendron. The driver of the buggy had run the wagon off the road and into a ditch. Eight of the marchers were trying to lift the wagon onto the road. The nurses had climbed out of the seat, and the driver was trying to calm the horses. The man in the buckboard had gone to the front of the marchers and was trying to make a speech from his buggy.

"I swear it's the truth," he shouted. "Mother Jones got a telegram from the president of the United States. If you turn back now and don't go into Logan, Pres. Warren Harding will listen to what you have to say."

"Show me the telegram," a voice commanded.

"Nobody listened to Sid Hatfield and he was murdered," an angry voice shouted.

Disgruntled threats to move or be shot brought one last plea from the man. "You've got to believe me. If you go on, it will be all out war. If you turn back now the government will be on your side."

"Move that coward. The president didn't help Sid, I'm ready for war," threatened the miners.

The horse was unhitched from the buggy and the driver and buggy hoisted by the angry mob and tossed off the road. The driver scampered from the overturned buggy and ran back down the road. The sergeant shouted several commands, and the miners fell back in line to continue their journey. The nurses climbed onto the seat of the supply wagon, while the driver walked along side the horses to keep them calm.

Brad ordered, "This is it. Let me do the talking. Let's go."

We followed Brad as he ran toward the supply wagon calling for help. One of the nurses heard his cries and called to the driver to stop the horses. The three of us grabbed the back of the wagon as Brad began his tale of woe.

"Please, ma'am," Brad begged, "please help us. We were thrown off the Powhatan Arrow in Charleston. We're just poor, and we're trying to get to our grandmother's in Logan. Could we ride a piece with you ladies?"

The short, stocky nurse eyed us suspiciously. "Do your parents know where you are?" she asked.

Brad bowed his head. "That's the problem. Our mom died of the fever and our pa got into some union trouble. We didn't have any kin in Charleston so we're trying to get to Grandma's," he said.

She softened and said, "Your pa was a union man?"

Brad replied, "Yes, ma'am."

"What's your name, son?" the nurse continued.

"Brown, ma'am, Brad Brown," answered Brad. "This is my sister Chelsea and my cousin Ginny," he replied, nodding in our direction.

She looked at the driver. "You ever hear of any Browns mixed up with the union?"

The driver removed his hat, scratched his head and mumbled, "I recollect some Browns living in Little Russia, but I don't rightly know if they were union folks or not."

"You climb right up here," offered the younger nurse as she moved crates and extended a helping hand.

"Cathy," replied the older woman, "this isn't a safe place for children. Maybe we should just leave them with the sheriff in Madison."

"Ann," Cathy said confidently, "we've got to help the kids get to their grandmother's. Who else can they turn to?"

Ann sighed and smiled. "You really want to take care of the whole world, don't you?"

"No," Cathy chuckled, "just my little corner of it."

Ann reached down to help Chelsea on board, while Cathy moved two more crates to make room for me. The driver, who came around back to see what was happening, made room for Brad behind the driver's seat. Cathy opened a crate filled with green woolen army blankets. She pulled out two; one she handed to Brad and the other to Chelsea and me.

"I have some extra shoes with me," she said. "In the morning I'll see if I can't fit you girls with something for your feet. Brad, I'm sure I'll be able to find something for you from some of the miners."

"Here," Ann offered as she handed a shoebox filled with sandwiches and cookies to Brad. "Help yourself and then pass these back to the girls. It's all we have until morning. We'll ride all night, set up a hospital tent in the morning, and then we'll fix you some breakfast."

"We need to get moving," cautioned the driver. "The miners are quite a piece up in front of us."

"We're ready now," said Cathy as she and Ann climbed onto the seat next to the driver.

Ann turned sideways and warned, "If you hear gunfire, keep your heads down. If Cathy or I tell you to run, do it immediately, and don't ask questions. Hide away from the wagon in the woods, and stay there until one of us comes looking for you."

We nodded and answered, "Yes, ma'am."

The driver slapped the reins, and the horses pulled the wagon with a jerk. The wagon wheels dug into the soft mud and slowly began to creak. The bed of the wagon swayed as the back wheels raised over the rocks and plunged into the ruts. The crates shifted from time to time and pushed me against the side of the wagon or toward Chelsea. After a while I wedged a part of the blanket between two crates and managed to use the lower crate as a pillow. I ate a lukewarm bologna and mustard sandwich on dry, stale bread, as the stars began to appear in the night sky. It seemed strange looking at the stars; this was August 1921, and the North Star and the Evening Star looked the same. I guess some things never change. I sat up to share my discovery with Chelsea, but she was fast asleep. I peered over the crates at Brad and saw him slumped behind the seat with his head resting on his chest. Ann and Cathy whispered to each other occasionally, and in the distance a faint chant from the marching miners could be heard over the creaking wagon wheels. I thought about home and wished I was back with Mom, Dad, and even David. This time-traveling stuff had been okay, but what if I never got back to them? Would Mom cry as much over me as she did over Grandpa? Would Kim miss me? At least I wouldn't have to worry about having Mrs. Hendrix for Algebra next year. Who knows, there might not be another next year. I bet David will really feel rotten for all the names he called me. Mom will never know how proud I was of her . . . when the . . .

"Wake up, sleepyheads," Cathy ordered cheerfully. "As soon as we unload the wagon, we'll whip up a good breakfast. How about bacon, eggs, biscuits, and red eye gravy?"

"Oh," moaned Chelsea, holding her head. "I don't want any red . . . I don't want any eyes."

My neck was stiff, my stomach was growling, and my clothes were damp from the heavy dew. I rubbed my eyes and stretched my arms high above my head. The sun filtered through the treetops and danced across the dew on the swaying leaves. The air was cool and filled with the moist smell of rich dirt. I unfolded my legs and tried to stretch my body from a sitting position between the crates.

"Let me help you down from the back of this high wagon," offered the driver as he extended both hands.

He lifted me down and then helped Chelsea. Brad was busy helping two miners, about his age, unload the crates. They stacked the crates to form makeshift walls underneath a canvas canopy. Ann directed the young men in forming the walls and setting up cots. Cathy stretched a large sheet with a red cross on it across one of the walls.

"I guess we're about ready for customers," Cathy signed. "This is one time I really don't want any."

"Are they going to have a real war?" I asked.

"About as real as war can get," answered Ann.

"Why?" I questioned.

"If your daddy was a union man, you shouldn't need to ask that question," Ann replied.

"I know the miners haven't been treated fairly," I began "but couldn't they complain to the sheriff or the governor? The president said he would listen."

"The sheriffs and governors are elected by the mine owners. They do what they're told to do. That's why the sheriff will arrest a miner if he goes on strike or refuses to work. And about the telegram from President Harding, I'm like the men. I'll believe it when I see it," Cathy explained.

"Hmp," snorted the driver. "The last word I heard on Harding was he was sending federal troops from Fort Thomas, Kentucky and a squadron of bombers from Langley Field in Virginia. He thinks . . . "

Chelsea interrupted, "Why would President Harding do that?

120

"He calls it keeping peace and protecting the property of citizens," the driver responded.

"It's more like keeping the miners enslaved to the coal companies and protecting the property of the wealthy mine owner," Ann added.

"Why are the miners here? Why don't they march on Washington?" I asked.

"Because their families and homes are here. They need to protect them," Cathy replied.

"How do you explain to a bigwig in Washington that you don't want to go down in a mine if it has gas? He doesn't even know what a coal mine looks like. How do you explain to one of them rich senators or representatives that you can't buy your kid shoes unless the company store has them in stock, and then they charge you double for the shoes. I'm telling you it can't be done. We go after the mine operators. Yes sir, that's what we're going to do. Right here on Blair Mountain," the driver said passionately.

"Do you think fighting the mine operators will make it better?" I asked.

"We're fighting for the right to have a union," the driver explained. "The right to freedom of assembly, just like it says in the Constitution."

"If the miners could form a union, the union would make certain agreements with the mine owners," Ann replied. "The union would offer one contract for all miners asking for eight-hour work days, safer working conditions, wages paid in real money, and protection from being fired for no reason at all."

Chelsea remarked, "That makes sense to me."

"If the miners can cross Blair Mountain and go into Logan County to form a union, they will win. If Don Chaffin's men, the Baldwin-Felts detectives, and the federal troops stop them . . . I guess we'll all be arrested and thrown in jail." Cathy added.

"Enough of this talk," Ann remarked. "We'd better eat before any real trouble begins. Brad, will you and Billy gather some firewood? Build a fire in front of the tent, and I'll get some hot food a cooking."

"Anything you say," Brad agreed as he and Billy jumped to their newly assigned duty.

"What would you like for me to do?" I asked.

"See the crate on top of the one marked bandages? I think I packed the iron skillets and the coffee pot in that one. Would you dig those out for me?" Ann asked.

121

"Chelsea," Cathy said, passing her a pail, "there's a little creek at the bottom of the hill. We'll need some water. Junior, you take these other two pails and go with her."

We hurried to our assigned chores. Within minutes the fire was blazing, and breakfast was cooking. I never realized bacon and even coffee could smell so good.

"Did you hear that?" Cathy asked.

Everyone froze in place. The bacon sizzled, the fire crackled, and the coffeepot bubbled and hissed as the boiling coffee dripped into the flames.

Ann whispered, "What sound?"

It seemed like hours before Cathy remarked, "That hum. Listen . . . there it is again."

The hum grew louder and louder. The eight of us stood in place without making a sound or moving a muscle. The hum grew to a roar as the shadow of a plane washed over the ground. All eyes focused on the sky as a squadron of Martin Bombers followed by six Army Air Corps planes flew overhead. A series of three explosions, followed by a barrage of rifle fire, ripped through the forest.

"Girls," Ann ordered, "get under the canopy and stay there. If you young men know how to use a rifle, they're in the back of the wagon. Cathy, you stay here and wait for the wounded. I'll take Seth with me since he handles the wagon so well. We'll go as close to the front line as possible to haul any wounded back who can't walk on their own."

"Be careful, Ann," pleaded Cathy.

"Don't worry; even mine owners respect a white uniform," replied Ann.

Seth hitched up the horses while Ann gathered bandages, morphine, and syringes. She stored her gear securely under the seat as Seth called to the horses and slapped the reins. Chelsea and I ran for the canopy. I knelt behind a crate marked bandages and searched the area for Brad. He stood between Billy and Junior, each holding a rifle. Chelsea moved away from the entrance and nearer to me.

"I don't like this," I remarked.

"I'm ready to leave," Chelsea whimpered.

"Brad, in here!" I yelled.

"Why isn't he coming?" Chelsea mumbled.

"Brad, hurry . . . "

A machine gun mounted on a nearby tree sent a series of rapid shots through the air. I thought someone was throwing firecrackers until I saw the dirt fly from around Brad's feet. Billy and Junior ran for cover, but Brad stood frozen in place.

Chelsea screamed, "Brad, Brad!"

"Stay here," I ordered. I ran from behind the crate into the clearing. Crisp popping sounds filled my ears, as Billy and Junior answered with zings from their rifles. Small puffs of smoke caused my eyes to water and the sharp smell of sulfur burned my nose and throat.

I reached for Brad's arm and screamed, "Hurry! Get back in the tent!"

He turned and stared at me but didn't move. I was frightened by his blank expression. He acted like he didn't recognize me. I took both his hands and tried to say calmly, "Brad, you need to come with me back to the tent."

Tears were running down his cheeks, but he didn't answer. He moved his feet, one at a time, as I pulled him gently toward the canvas canopy. He stared at me as if I were some alien from outer space.

When we were about ten feet from the makeshift hospital, Chelsea ran out to meet us. She threw her arms around Brad's neck. He stood motionless.

"Chelsea," I demanded, "help me get him inside."

We each grabbed an arm and pulled Brad as he walked stiffly into the tent. We sat him down on one of the army cots away from the entrance. Tears continued to run down his cheeks, but he made no sound.

Cathy came rushing back with a pan of water and a damp cloth. "He's okay, girls. Don't worry. He's just a little shook up," she remarked as she gently began to bathe his face with the cool water. "It's not everyday someone tries to kill you."

"Oh, Ginny!" Chelsea cried. "I hate it! I hate it! I wish we had never found that stupid horseshoe! What if . . . "

I put my arms around Chelsea and moved her quickly toward the front of the open tent behind the crates. "Chelsea, he's okay. You heard Cathy; he's just shaken up a bit," I said softly.

Sounds of exploding grenades, zinging rifles, and popping machine guns mingled with human yells and cries. I reached into my pocket for the horseshoe and pulled it out.

"I'm ready," I said. "How about you?"

"I've been ready. Let's get out of here." Chelsea said.

Cathy came toward us with the pan of water and cloth. She threw the dirty water out the front of the tent. "Brad will feel better . . . "

Boom! The ground shook. Two of the supply crates tumbled open on the ground as dirt flew everywhere. One of the poles holding the canopy fell, and a lantern crashed to the ground. Billy and Junior rushed inside and began restacking the crates at the entrance.

Cathy rushed to set the pole upright. "That was too close. You girls move toward the back and check on Brad. Ann will probably be coming back soon with the wounded. I'll need you to help up front then."

We nodded and headed toward Brad. I knelt next to the cot and held the horseshoe upright.

I gasped, "They're gone. All the diamonds are gone."

Chelsea grabbed the horseshoe and turned it over and over in her hand. "How will it pick up light? Ginny, we'll never get out of here," she whispered.

I took the horseshoe from Chelsea and slipped between two crates toward a ray of sunlight. I held the horseshoe up to the light. There was no sparkle, not even a gleam. I rubbed my thumb and fingers over the empty gold and felt the hollowed pits that once held the magnificent jewels. They were gone.

I darted between the crates and back to the cot. I grabbed Brad's shoulders and began to shake him. "Wake up, wake up, you've got to wake up." My voice seemed to echo in my ears.

Someone, maybe Chelsea or Cathy, was holding my arms. The horseshoe dropped. Oh, no, I had to find it. There wasn't much time left. The gun sounds were louder. There was a hum, more planes were flying overhead. The sunlight, I could feel it. It was bright and warm, but where was the horseshoe? Every time I reached down to find it, someone held my arms.

"Chelsea, help me, Chelsea," I pleaded. "It's here; I know it's here."

I could see it, there on the ground in front of me. I reached for the horseshoe just as Cathy stopped me. "Let me go!" I screamed. "Let me go!"

I pushed and shoved, but Cathy wouldn't let go of my arms. Suddenly Ann appeared. Was she back with the wounded already?

Facts

1. Mary "Mother" Jones became an organizer for the United Mine Workers in 1891. In 1902 she entered West Virginia to help organize the Kanawha, New River, and Pocahontas fields. In 1921, at the age of ninety-one, she tried to keep the miners from entering Logan and Mingo counties by way of Blair Mountain.

2. "Two-Gun" Sid Hatfield, a union organizer, was charged with murder in the Matewan Massacre. He was killed in August 1921 on the courthouse steps in Welch, West Virginia, when he appeared to stand trial. His murder prompted the miners to march on Logan for the right to form unions.

3. On August 24, 1921, an army of about three thousand miners met at Marmet in Kanawha County. The miners, many of whom were veterans of World War I, arranged the march in military fashion. They divided into units, used modern weapons of warfare, seized railroad trains, purchased supplies, and were accompanied by physicians and nurses.

4. The first week in September the miners arrived on Blair Mountain and faced about twelve hundred men. The two forces battled along a twenty-five mile front. The miners faced federal troops from Fort Thomas, Kentucky, and a squadron of bombers from Langley Field, Virginia. The miners surrendered on September 4 when the regular army plus the Army Air Corps began dropping bombs.

5. Three deputy sheriffs were killed and about forty defenders were wounded, but the number of killed or wounded miners is not known. Five hundred and forty-three miners were held for trial, and twenty-two leaders were charged with treason against the state.

6. The coalfields of West Virginia during the 1800s and early 1900s were controlled by the "company." The miners worked in unsafe conditions twelve or more hours a day and were paid only twenty-five cents for each carload of coal. Explosions, cave-ins, slate falls, and gas and water-filled mines were commonplace.

7. Miners and their families had to live in company houses, shop

125

at the company store, and were paid in scrip. By paying miners with scrip the company made sure that miners could only purchase goods from the coal company.

8. Any miner complaining about these conditions would be fired, evicted from his home, and then placed on a blacklist. This list would be given to all companies and the miner would not be hired anywhere.

9. Some companies insisted miners sign "yellow dog" contracts. By signing this contract, a miner would agree not to join a union. If he did, he would automatically be fired.

Chapter 8

Home at Last

"Call Dr. McDowell," Cathy told Ann as she gently pushed my shoulders down on the pillow.

"Do you think she'll need a sedative?" asked Ann, standing at the foot of the bed.

"I don't know. Just get Dr. McDowell."

Ann disappeared through the doorway. The doorway? What happened to the tent? I was in a room! The white ceiling above me had acoustic panels with recessed fluorescent lighting. The pale pink walls were accented with floral drapes pulled open to let the warm sunlight flood the room. I was strapped on to a hospital bed with my head and feet slightly elevated. There was one overstuffed plastic chair in the corner and the movable tray stand was pushed against the wall.

"Cathy, where am I?"

"You're in the Welch Emergency Hospital." she said. "A lot of people are going to be thrilled that you've finally come around."

"What do you mean, 'come around'?"

"I'll let Dr. McDowell tell you that," Cathy answered with a smile.

"Haven't we met before?" I asked.

"I've been your nurse all week. But I didn't realize you knew my name until just a few minutes ago," replied Cathy. "I guess that subconscious mind is always at work."

"Where's my mom? Does she know where I am?"

"Certainly. She brought you in five days ago." Cathy said.

"Where is she now?"

"I'll notify her as soon as Dr. McDowell gets here. I'm sure she and your father will be right over," Cathy assured me.

"My dad? What's he doing here?"

"You've been a very sick young lady," Cathy explained. "Your father and brother flew in two days ago. They were just in . . . "

"Good morning, Sleeping Beauty," boomed a man's voice as the door flew open. "It's about time you decided to come back to the real world." The tall, lanky man with thick glasses moved over to the bed and stood smiling down at me.

"Ginny, this is Dr. McDowell. He'll explain to you what has happened. I'll go right now and call your parents." Cathy patted me on the hand and left the room.

The doctor put on his stethoscope and listened to my heart and lungs. He hummed some song to himself as he pulled a penlight from his pocket. "I want to see if your pretty green eyes can follow this light. Ann, would you turn off the lights and close the drapes, please?"

I watched as Ann followed the doctor's orders. When she moved to the other side of my bed, I asked, "What about the miners? Were many of them wounded?"

Ann looked puzzled; then she smiled at me and at the doctor. "They're fine. Don't you worry about them."

"You been dreaming about miners, huh?" Dr. McDowell commented as he turned on the tiny penlight. "Now you look straight ahead, don't watch the light." He flipped a small shield over his left eye and moved the light up in my face.

I felt so mixed up. These people were silently laughing at me. *They thought I was nuts. He's probably looking for a brain in my head and can't find one. I guess Mom is upset. Why did I have to get sick now? She called Dad. I hope he isn't mad because he had to fly to West Virginia. I wonder what the doctor meant when he said I was dreaming about miners? I doubt if he is a real doctor. He looks more like that reporter we ran into at Harpers Ferry. I'll ask Cathy about the miners when she comes back,* I thought.

"Ginny, Ginny." Ann spoke softly as she shook my shoulders. "Do you feel like sitting up now?"

"Sure," I responded as I tried to sit up. I had such a strange sensation. I was telling my brain to sit me up, but my body wasn't moving. *Come on, move.* I kept telling myself. *This is dumb. You've got to sit up. Something really bad must be wrong with me. I'm going to die. That's why Dad is here. I'm going to die!* I began to cry.

"Let me help you," Ann offered, as she slid one arm under my shoulders and pulled me forward.

Dr. McDowell asked, "Why the tears? You appear to be in good health to me."

"You're no doctor. You're a reporter," I whimpered and continued to cry.

"My mother would be furious if she heard you say that," laughed Dr. McDowell. "Trust me, after eight years of medical school and twelve years of private practice, I am a doctor. And you, young lady, are in good health. That acute infection in the middle ear has cleared up, you have regained consciousness, and your vital signs are all stable. I think a few hamburgers, couple of large fries, and a soda would be the best medicine for you now. Ann, would you order . . ."

The door behind Dr. McDowell flew open and the lights were switched on. Mom and Dad came rushing toward the bed. Mom was crying as she hugged and kissed me. She held me in her arms and rocked back and forth. Dad was talking softly to Dr. McDowell as they shook hands.

"Mom, I'm okay. Really I am."

"Oh, Ginny." she wiped her eyes. "I think this trip has been a horrible mistake. I can hardly wait to get home."

Dr. McDowell left the room along with Ann when Dad approached the bed. "How's my all-star?" he asked, giving me a big hug and a kiss.

"I'm all right, I guess. I just can't remember much. Did David come with you?" I asked.

"Yes and no," replied Dad. "He's here in West Virginia, but he stayed with your grandmother this morning."

"Just as I expected. He doesn't care if I live or die," I mumbled.

"He'll be along later. We didn't all want to barge in on you at once," Dad continued, "Dr. McDowell said he'd like to keep you here for observation during the next twenty-four hours; then it's California here we come."

"No," Mom interrupted, "she'll need a few days of rest before the trip back. We'll leave on Wednesday. That will give her at least two days to visit with Chelsea and Brad. She only saw them for a few hours last Saturday night."

"What do you mean, a few hours? We've been all over this state!" I exclaimed.

Mom and Dad exchanged glances. Then Mom patted my hand.

129

"Ginny, you've been in the hospital for over five days. Honey, you haven't been anywhere. Do you remember when you were small and you used to have those terrible earaches? Something about the air pressure on the plane trip here caused the tubes in your ears to become clogged and infected. Dear, you've been unconscious for the last five days."

I glanced up at Dad and he nodded his head in agreement. "Mom, did Chelsea, Brad, and I find an old trunk in the coal bin at Grandma's house?"

"Yes." Mom beamed as she smiled at Dad. "You do remember finding the trunk?"

"Was there a horseshoe in the trunk? A golden horseshoe with sapphires and diamonds?" I asked.

"Ginny, I'm so surprised that you remember all this," Mom commented. "Dr. McDowell told us you would experience a period of amnesia. I can't believe you recall finding that trunk, let alone the golden horseshoe."

I answered, "I remember all right, especially the horseshoe. We've had it all . . . " I paused and then asked, "Where is the horseshoe now?"

"The director of the Cultural Museum in Charleston picked it up late yesterday. It will stay there on exhibit," Mom explained. "Your grandmother donated the diary and infant's clothing to the museum, too."

"What about the other things?"

"Chelsea and Brad picked out a keepsake for themselves. Chelsea picked out a l . . . Chelsea picked out something special for you, but I'll let her give that to you when she comes to visit."

"I can't believe she's not up here already," Dad remarked. "She was tickled to death when we got the call this morning that you had regained consciousness."

Mom chuckled, "There's a new man in Chelsea's life. It seems that Mrs. Barry has a foreign exchange student that just arrived from England."

"England," Dad remarked. "I thought he was from France?"

"No, England," Mom continued. "He just has a French name—Dominick."

I sat upright on my own. "Dominick, he's here?" I exclaimed.

Mom and Dad exchanged puzzled looks. Mom frowned and continued, "Do you know someone named Dominick?"

How did I answer that? I fumbled for words, "Well, not exactly. Chelsea talked about him the first night after we got here."

"Oh," Mom muttered. "I thought he just arrived on Tuesday. I can't keep up with all the boys Chelsea talks about."

"Did I hear my name?" called a cheery voice as Chelsea bounced into the room. She flashed a warm smile and rushed to give me a bouquet of balloons tied with twirling pastel ribbons.

"They're beautiful!" I shouted, hugging Chelsea. My eyes fell on the heavy black ribbon that held Chelsea's thick dark curls. "Where did you get that ribbon?" I asked.

"Oh, I guess you don't remember," began Chelsea. "You see, we found this old trunk . . . "

"I remember that part. Where did you get that ribbon?"

"It was in the trunk," Chelsea answered. "It's just a plain old ribbon. I didn't see anything so great about it, but this guy I met . . . I can hardly wait to tell you about Dominick. He's from England. Well, he thought the ribbon would look nice in my hair. So I tried it, and everyone seems to like it. Ginny, now I know this sounds stupid, but I get the strangest feeling when I tie this ribbon in my hair. It's hard to explain . . . you know."

Dad rolled his eyes and glanced at Mom. "What do you say, shall we go back, so David can have the car to come and visit?"

Mom nodded and leaned over to kiss me good-bye. "You two go ahead with your girl talk. We'll be back later, dear. We love you, Ginny."

"You'll never know how happy we were to get that phone call this morning. You take care of yourself. We'll see you around two-thirty this afternoon," Dad whispered as he kissed me good-bye.

"Don't worry about a thing," chattered Chelsea. "I'll just catch her up on the latest news about Brad and his old girl friend, Sarah."

Mom and Dad waved and then left the room. Before the door closed, Ann came in carrying a tray with oatmeal, biscuits, milk, and country ham, and scrambled eggs. "It's a little too early in the morning for hamburgers and fries, so I brought you this instead. If you want to try some red eye gravy I'll have the cafeteria send some right up."

Chelsea blurted, "Red eye what? Yuk! That sounds awful."

"I want to try it, Ann," I requested. "I think it's made with bacon drippings and coffee. It smelled pretty good . . . "

"You eat that kind of stuff in California?" asked Chelsea.

"No, if I remember correctly *you* eat that kind of stuff in West Virginia," I retorted.

131

Chelsea shrugged. "Suit yourself. Personally I don't care for anything that doesn't come out of a box or a can."

"Yes, I know. And your favorite way to cook food is to nuke it in the microwave."

"Trust me, cousin," laughed Chelsea. "It's the best way."

"Tell me about Sarah," I said as I sprinkled sugar over the oatmeal and began to eat.

"Well, sweet, sweet, I mean, *honey-dripping sweet,*" mocked Chelsea in a slow southern drawl, "little Sarah is back in town. She's so sweet I get a cavity just listening to her talk. Brad follows her around like a whipped puppy. It's disgusting, I tell you. Now granted, she is pretty, not beautiful or gorgeous, just pretty. But so dumb and shallow. Her idea of a cultural evening is watching live arena wrestling."

I laughed. "You've got to be kidding."

"I swear it's the truth," said Chelsea, holding up her right hand.

"Would her father happen to be the local sheriff?" I asked.

"Yes, but how did you know that?"

"Does she have blue eyes, long blonde hair, and drink a lot of lemonade with ice?" I continued to probe.

A confused Chelsea replied, "Yes, yes, and I don't know about the lemonade. How do you know so much? Wait, instead of amnesia, you have ESP. This is great. We can make big bucks by you telling fortunes."

I smiled. "I'm not telling you the future. I'm telling you about the time trips with the golden horseshoe."

Chelsea laughed, "Time trips. Come on, Ginny, get real."

I sat up and pushed the bed tray away from me. I motioned for Chelsea to move nearer the bed. "Chelsea, I mean it. You, Brad, and I traveled back in time. We were captured by some mound builders . . . "

Chelsea stepped back, wide-eyed, away from the bed. "Now look, Ginny, I don't know what kind of drugs they put you on in this place. You might have taken a trip, I think you're still on it; but Brad and I haven't been anywhere."

"Chelsea," I protested, "you've got to believe me. If we weren't on Blair Mountain with Cathy and Ann, how did I recognize them? If we hadn't gone to Harpers Ferry, how could I have described Sarah to you or known about her dad?"

"For Pete's sake, Ginny," Chelsea retaliated, "these nurses have been around you all week. You probably heard them talking to each other before you woke up this morning. And Sarah's dad has been sheriff for two hundred years. You've heard the name before, I'm sure. As far as Sarah being a blonde, that's a lucky guess."

Tears began to roll down my cheeks. "Maybe I am crazy and just dreamed all this garbage," I muttered.

"I'm sorry, Gin," Chelsea pleaded. "I'm sorry. I didn't mean to upset you. Wait, I brought you something. Remember when we were going through the trunk? Well, later when the director of the museum came, we dug through it again. Grandma gave her lots of things for the museum, and Brad and I got to select something for us. Brad picked the ugliest pair of red suspenders that I have ever seen. Of course, Brad never did have good taste. You can tell that by the girls he dates."

The door to my room opened and Cathy came in carrying a tiny pill cup. She smiled at me as she poured a cup of water from the Styrofoam pitcher next to my bed. "Dr. McDowell doesn't want you to overdo it today. This is just a mild sedative; you may feel a little drowsy in a few minutes," she explained when she handed me the small oval pink pill.

"Thanks," I said, placing the pill on the back of my tongue and swallowing. "I may as well be asleep. No one seems to listen to what I have to say."

"Oh, Gin," said Chelsea, "I've been listening. It's just . . . well the things you're saying seem a little odd. Hey, it's the medicine . . . "

"Your fever was extremely high the past few days. Sometimes that causes a person to hallucinate. But don't worry, you're going to be just fine," commented Cathy.

"Tell me the truth, Chelsea," I asked. "Do you think time travel is possible?"

"I don't know," pondered Chelsea. "Ginny, I don't even think about these kind of things. What's the point in it?"

"The point is I'm not crazy! I did travel in time, and you and Brad were with me," I insisted.

"Just how do you intend to prove it?" Chelsea snapped back.

"Have I ever seen Dominick?" I asked.

"No."

"Has my mom?"

"Not that I know of," Chelsea said.

"Have you described him to me?" I continued.

"What is this, twenty questions?"

"I'm trying to prove to you that we did travel in time. Now answer

133

the question. Have you described or shown me any pictures of Dominick?'' I insisted.

"No, your honor, I have not described or shown you any pictures of Dominick," mocked Chelsea.

"Dominick is your age, average build, and has long dark hair. He is very proper and dignified. His father is wealthy, likes to read books, has composed music for the cello . . . and likes to experiment with chemicals. His mother writes poetry, rides horses . . . ''

"Stop it," Chelsea whispered. She stared at me a long time and stammered, "This is scary. Ginny, how do you know all those things?''

"Chelsea," I began, "that's what I've been trying to tell you. The grown-ups will think I've flipped out; I'm not even going to try to explain it to them."

Chelsea pulled the green plastic chair to the side of the bed and sat down. "Explain, explain this time business or whatever you keep talking about."

"It started with the horseshoe, you know, the one we found in the trunk," I said.

Chelsea nodded. "Go on."

"Somehow when I was holding it, it began to glow and spin. It got away from me and I tried to grab it," I explained.

"Ginny, remember what that nurse said about hallucinating?" said Chelsea. "I think she's right. I was with you when you were holding the horseshoe. It did not glow, spin, or fly away."

"It did glow and spin! It did!" I screamed.

Chelsea jumped up, frightened, just as Cathy came running in the door.

"Take it easy; calm down," Cathy said, easing me back against the pillows. "Maybe you should leave now," she said to Chelsea. "It's been a long week for Ginny, and she doesn't need anymore excitement."

"I-I'm sorry," remarked Chelsea. "I didn't mean to upset you, Gin. Hey, I'll come back later, okay?''

I nodded and closed my eyes. This middle ear problem must really mess with your mind. I guess it was just one long dream.

"Oh, wait. I almost forgot!" exclaimed Chelsea. "We picked this out for you."

I opened my eyes, as Chelsea placed a tarnished silver locket in my hand. The lid had etched roses . . . "I'll see you later. Don't go anywhere until I get back," teased Chelsea. She waved good-bye.

"What a beautiful locket," Cathy remarked softly. "Would you want to wear it? I'll help you put it on."

"Open it first and tell me if there are any pictures inside. Would you, please?"

Cathy opened the locket and handed it to me. Sure enough, it was Sadie and Devil Anse. How could I get anyone to believe me? I know I really traveled. I kept trying to think of ways to convince Chelsea that she was with me, but I was so tired.

"Cathy, do you believe in time travel?" I whispered. "Have you ever been to a place called Blair Mountain?"

Cathy winked and patted my hand. "Junior and Billy will tell you all about it."